Cajun Folktales

Cajun Folktales

J.J. Reneaux

August House Publishers, Inc.
L I T T L E · R O C K

© 1992 by J.J. Reneaux.
All rights reserved. This book, or parts thereof,
may not be reproduced in any form without permission.
Published by August House, Inc.,
P.O. Box 3223, Little Rock, Arkansas, 72203,
501-372-5450.

Printed in the United States of America

10 9 8 7 6 5 4 3 2 1

LIBRARY OF CONGRESS CATALOGING-IN-PUBLICATION DATA
Reneaux, J.J., 1955–
Cajun folktales / J.J. Reneaux. — 1st ed.
p.   cm.
Summary: a collection of twenty-seven traditional Cajun tales, including animal stories,
fairy tales, ghost stories, and humorous tales.
ISBN 0-87483-283-7 (hb) : $19.95
ISBN 0-87483-282-9 (pb) : $9.95
1. Tales—Louisiana.   2. Cajuns—Folklore.
[1. Folklore—Louisiana.   2. Cajuns—Folklore.]   I. Title.
PZ8.1.R278Caj   1992
398.2'09763—dc20   92-18627

First Edition, 1992

Executive editor: Liz Parkhurst
Project editor: Kathleen Harper
Design director: Ted Parkhurst
Cover design: Bill Jennings
Typography: Lettergraphics / Little Rock

This book is printed on archival-quality paper which meets the
guidelines for performance and durability of the Committee on
Production Guidelines for Book Longevity of the
Council on Library Resources.

AUGUST HOUSE, INC.   PUBLISHERS   LITTLE ROCK

pour les Cadiens partout

Acknowledgments

The idea for this book was conceived during my year as a visiting artist in North Carolina. I gratefully acknowledge Mrs. Augusta Hyde, Mr. Jimmy Neil Smith, and Mr. Gene Champagne for their kind assistance at various stages of this work. Special thanks to Dr. Max Reinhart for his thorough proofreading of the manuscript, and to my editor, Kathleen Harper, for her energy and enthusiasm. Finally, my undying gratitude to all the good people who shared the gift of story with me through the years.

Contents

Introduction   *11*

Animal Tales   *15*

Why Alligator Hates Dog   *17*
M'su Lion Makes a Big Mistake   *21*
M'su Carencro and Mangeur de Poulet   *24*
The Theft of Honey   *26*

Fairy Tales   *31*

Catafo and the Devil   *33*
King Peacock   *40*
Baptiste and the Pirates   *48*
Julie and Julien   *54*
Jean Malin and the Bull-Man   *66*
Marie Jolie   *73*
The Magic Gifts   *81*

Funny Folk Tales   *87*

Po' Boy and the Ten Thousand Dollar Egg   *89*
Why La Graisse (Grease) Lives in the Kitchen   *95*
An Honest Man   *101*
Jean Sot and Bull's Milk   *106*
Jean Sot and the Giant Cows   *111*
St. Antoine the Wonder Worker   *116*
Roclore and His Bag of Tricks   *120*
The Killer Mosquitoes   *124*
Pierre and the Angel of Death   *128*
Dead Men Don't Talk   *133*

Ghost Stories   *139*

Fifolet   *141*
The Half-Man   *145*
The Ghost of Jean Lafitte   *149*
Knock, Knock, Who's There?   *153*
The Singing Bones   *158*
The Ring and the Rib   *165*

Glossary   *172*

Introduction

In the early 1760s the first Acadians began to arrive in French Louisiana after their tragic forced migration from what is now Ile de Prince Edward, New Brunswick, and Nova Scotia, Canada. They brought with them only tools, clothing, cooking pots—their barest possessions. But in order to survive in this strange land they would need more than just practical things. The Acadians, better known as the Cajuns, also brought with them a deep faith in *le Bon Dieu* and a rich heritage of songs and stories.

Their new home presented great challenges. They had to adjust to a subtropical climate, a diet of strange plants and animals, the harsh realities of life on the frontier. They encountered foreign customs and peculiar superstitions. Even their language was challenged. Here was a whole world of unfamiliar plant and animal life, terrain, life style, beliefs—experiences and concepts for which their own language had no equivalent.

The Cajun people had withstood persecution, the loss of their homeland, hunger, disease, and the deaths and separation of family and friends. But like the tree that bends with the wind that would break it, they adapted with spirit and ingenuity. The old ways that were still useful they kept; those that were not they abandoned in favor of new ways of working and living, borrowing freely from the crafts and languages of the African, Indian, Spanish, and Anglo peoples that populated colonial Louisiana. They eventually learned how to squeeze a living from the swamps, bayous, and prairies, and how to get along with snakes, mosquitoes, heat, and hurricanes.

In time, the Cajuns modified their own stories to suit their adopted homeland. Kings came to live on bayous; princesses ate *couche-couche* and gumbo; the great northern *loup-garou* prowled the swamps. African motifs gradually blended into the Cajun melting pot; comic animal characters like the trickster Lapin and his dull-witted companion Bouqui wrestled over human-like problems, bringing laughter to the Cajuns' hard lives. Influences from Indian and Spanish cultures added vocabulary, superstitions, and themes to Cajun folklore. The encounter with Anglo culture almost always produced humorous results, as in the misadventures of *les Americains* or newly arrived Europeans (especially Irishmen) as they tried to survive the baffling land of Louisiana. All of these elements combined with Cajun traditions, creating a gumbo of folklore that is unique in American culture.

In this collection I have attempted to offer a wide sampling of story types, divided roughly into four categories: fairy tales, animal stories, funny folk tales, ghost stories. Some of them are very old and little known today, while others may still be told on *galeries* or at bedtime to *les petits*. All of the stories derive from my life and experience. I heard most of them firsthand from family, neighbors, and friends in Louisiana and Southeast Texas. They were related in many different places on as many different occasions: fishing trips, fish frys, neighborhood *fais-dodos,* school playgrounds, holiday gatherings, the old ladies' *café au lait*-sippin' hen parties. Others I collected over the years from Cajun friends and acquaintances, not only in Louisiana but across the country as well, in the most varied of locations—airports, dances, nursing homes, schools. Young people usually told the stories in English, spicing them with a smattering of Cajun French. Older raconteurs often spoke in their beloved Cajun French, occasionally in Black French. I have included stories from this last category which, at least until recent years, were common fare among white and black French-speaking people in Louisiana and Southeast Texas.

Like any good raconteur, I have told the tales for true as I heard them, but added personal touches, twists, and turns as the stories grew to be a natural part of my own life. For me, these tales are not museum pieces whose time was and is no more. They are alive and vigorous, brimming with *joie de vivre,* the zest for life that is the essence of Cajun culture.

Thus each of these stories contains a part of me—the beliefs, experiences, and people who have shaped my life. I share these tales with love and pride. It is my hope that readers and listeners will discover the beauty and spirit of the Cajun people and—perhaps more importantly—of their own lives as well.

J.J. Reneaux

Animal Tales

Why Alligator Hates Dog

*When I was a little girl, flooding was a normal occurrence. Often after one of these downpours the kids would go out and catch crawfish with our neighbor, Mrs. Irene Guillery. Once a pretty good-sized alligator washed up into our ditch. Our hound dog, Bullet, set up an uproar, growling and barking till we all came running out to see what the ruckus was about. Alligator didn't seem especially bothered by us kids yelling and hollering, but he hissed and snapped at that dog like crazy. A couple of men came out and caught the gator and returned him to the swamp. Not long after that, I sat with Miss Irene as she sipped **café au lait** from a saucer, and explained to me why Alligator hates Dog.*

M'su Cocodrie, the alligator, was once king of all the swamp and the bayous. All the critters cut a wide circle 'round ol' Cocodrie lest they wind up in his belly. Even Man with his traps and guns was wary of M'su Cocodrie. One snap of those jaws and a fella could lose an arm, a leg, or even his life. M'su Cocodrie enjoyed the respect and fear of everybody—everybody, that is, except for *les chiens,* the dogs. How those dogs loved to tease and mock him—from a safe distance, of course!

Back in those days, M'su Cocodrie lived in a deep, dark, muddy hole in the bank of the bayou, not far from the *cabane* of Man and his pesky dogs. In the evening he loved to curl up in his hole and take a little nap before he went hunting for his supper. But just as he was dozing off, the dogs up at the *cabane* would start carryin' on, howlin', whinin', barkin', teasin', till he thought he'd go mad!

They'd howl out, "M'suuuu Cocodrie! M'suuuuu Cocodrie! Come and get us if you dare." And ooowhee! Alligator couldn't even do a thing about it, 'cept gnash those big ol' sharp teeth, thump his tail, and wait for one of those dogs to get just a little too close.

"One of these days I'm gonna get them dogs," he'd hiss. "I'll teach them to mock me, the King o' the Swamp!"

Now, one day Hound Dog came running down the bank of the bayou. I mean he was hot on the trail of Lapin, the rabbit. Thumpity, thumpity, thump. But that rabbit was too smart-smart. She led that dog right up to Alligator's hole. Well, Lapin easily jumped across, but Dog fell straight down that hole and found himself snout to snout with M'su Cocodrie. Hound Dog knew he was trapped and he better do some fast talkin' if he was gonna get out of there alive.

"Arrrhoooo," howled Hound Dog. *"Comment ça va? How's it goin'?"*

"Sooooo, at last you come to pay me a visit, hmmmm?" hissed Alligator. "Every evenin' you dogs call out, 'M'suuuu Cocodrie, come and get us!' Well, now, that's exactly what I'm gonna do. I'm gonna get you, and I'm gonna grind you into mincemeat, you miserable, mangy mutt!"

"Oh, *mais non, mon ami,*" whined Dog. "But no, my friend. Surely you did not think that my friends and I would insult you, the mighty King o' the Swamp. Oh, *mais jamais! Pas du tout!* We were only callin' you to join us for supper. We did not call out, 'Come and get us'—we called out, 'Come and get it, come and get it.' You see, every evenin' our master brings us a big bowl filled with delicious scraps of meat and bones. We call for you to come and get it, to come and join us for supper. But you never come, *mon padnat.*"

"Hmmm, is that so?" asks M'su Cocodrie.

"Oh, *mais oui!* Come this very evenin' and dine with us. For you, we will save the very best," says Dog.

"Hmm," says M'su Cocodrie, "but what of your master, the man?"

"Oh, do not worry about him. Us dogs will keep watch. If we see our master comin', we'll warn you in plenty of time and you can escape. Come and join us. We will save the very best scraps for you. After all, *mon ami,* shouldn't the King o' the Swamp eat as good as us poor dogs?"

Now, M'su Cocodrie was a powerful and fearsome creature, for sure. But he wasn't overly blessed with what you call the smarts. He thought with his stomach and he acted on the advice of his mighty appetite. So he agreed to come for supper, and he let that rascal, Dog, escape the crush of his jaws.

That evening Alligator crawled up the bank of the bayou all the way to the *cabane.* When he got to the steps of the *galerie,* the porch, he stopped and looked around, for he feared the master might be somewhere about. But the dogs started whinin', "Come up, come up, M'su Cocodrie. Our master is not here. Do you see our master? Do you hear our master? It is safe, M'su Cocodrie. You can have your pick o' the scraps. Come up and get it, M'su, come and get it!"

M'su Cocodrie looked for sure. He didn't see a thing. He listened and all was quiet. So he climbed up the steps to the *galerie,* draggin' that big, heavy tail behind him. But no sooner had he tasted one bite of those juicy scraps than the dogs started carrying on, howlin', whinin', barkin', teasin', and their master came running out to see what all the ruckus was about. When Man saw M'su Cocodrie on his porch, he took a club and started beating him on the snout, yelling for his wife to fetch his gun. And if that wasn't bad enough, those snarling dogs leaped on M'su Cocodrie and began to bite him on his tail. Poor Alligator was lucky to escape back down his hole with his life!

Well, ever since that time Alligator hates Dog. He floats in the water like a half-sunk log with only those big eyes peering out. He's waiting and watching for one of those dogs to come just a little too close. This time Dog won't be able to trick M'su Cocodrie. These days ol' Alligator is a lot smarter. He's learned his lesson. And if M'su Cocodrie were here today, why, he'd tell you himself, for true, "Believe nothin' you hear, *mon ami,* and only half of what you see, hmmmm?"

M'su Lion Makes A Big Mistake

*We have all met M'su Lion in person, in the form of folks who love to brag and boast. This story reminds me of a girl I knew in the third grade who bragged constantly on her shiny shoes, her naturally curly ringlets, and her ruffly dresses. One day there was an audition for the part of a wicked witch in the school's Halloween play. This prissy little girl tried out and she was just awful. I was shy and ashamed of my own hand-me-down clothing. But suddenly something happened: I got mad! I stood right up and told a tale I'd heard from my **maman** about a haunted house. When I finished, I looked out and nobody was laughing—they were right there with me in that haunted house. I didn't get the role of the witch but I did discover the power of storytelling.*

One morning M'su Lion was strutting through the woods when he met up with Mamselle Lapin, the rabbit. They stopped to shoot the breeze, and pretty soon Lion was just carrying on like he always did. "You know," brags Lion, "I'm the number one boss around here, ain't that the truth?"

"Oh, no," says Mamselle Rabbit, "you are not the boss at all." Just then she wiggled her nose, twitched her ears, and ran to hide in her hole.

Lion kept on strutting till he met up with M'su Ours, the bear. "Tell me," he asks, "ain't I the number one boss around here?"

"Oh no, you are not the boss at all," says Bear. "God is the boss in heaven, and Man is the boss on earth."

Lion growled and pawed the ground. "For true, God is the master above," he says, "but me, I'm the master down here!"

"Yeyiiee!" cries M'su Ours suddenly, full of fear. "Now is not the time to argue that question. Do you not see Man comin' with that awful-lookin' stick on his shoulder? I will let you and him decide who's boss." And Bear hurried off into the swamp woods.

Man came closer and closer. M'su Lion growled and pawed the ground, but Man kept on coming until he got about a hundred yards away. There he stopped and pointed his stick at Lion, and suddenly there was a big bang! Something hot hit M'su Lion upside the head. That hurt him bad, and he took off running. He was making tracks when he heard another blast. Something hot hit him in his rear. That hurt so bad he didn't stop running until he had left the path and run through the woods to hide on the river bank. There he stayed until he had licked his wounds and was hungry enough to come out.

It was dark when Lion came limping out with his tail between his legs. When he saw Bear again he calls out, "Eh! M'su Ours! Is that you?"

"Oui, c'est moi, it's me," says Bear with a sigh, for he had better things to do than listen to Mr. Big Mouth.

M'su Lion starts telling him all about his troubles. "Man didn't even give me a fair chance to fight him, man to beast," he complains. "He came up 'bout a hundred yards from me, and blam, blam, blam! I still don't know what hit me. Somethin' knocked me upside the head, like to've rattled my brains out. Then, when I was 'bout to attack 'im, somethin' hot smoked my rear! Well, that 'bout did it, and I got outta there quick-quick. I got to admit, Bear, you sure was right 'bout who's number one boss," says M'su Lion. "God is the boss above, and Man sure 'nuf is the boss below." But then Lion rares way up to his full height and roars, "But at least … I come in third!"

Bear says, "M'su Lion, you are the number three boss for true." And he went on his way, just laughing and thinking to himself, "Some folks surely are full of themselves!"

M'su Carencro and Mangeur de Poulet

*The late great king of Zydeco, Clifton Chênier, once said, "Be who you is!" If ever a story delivered that message, this is it. This tale speaks of the deep faith most Cajun people have in **le Bon Dieu**. It was a favorite with my neighbor of thirty years ago, Mr. Laurence Molleré.*

One day M'su Carencro, the buzzard, was sitting on a fence post real patient-like, just waiting for something to drop dead so he could have his supper, when who should come flapping up but ol' Mangeur de Poulet, the chicken hawk. Mangeur de Poulet calls out, "Hey, *ça va, mon padnat?*"

M'su Carencro shook his head and sighed, *"Ça va mal!* Not good at all! I am so hungry. I been waitin' for days for somethin' to drop dead so I can have my supper."

"What you talkin' 'bout?" says know-it-all Chicken Hawk. "If you're so hungry, why don'tcha get out there and hunt you some good fresh meat? You got eyes, you got wings, you got a beak. Go for it! You got to look out for Number One in this world, *mon ami.*"

"*Non, non, non,*" says Buzzard, "you don't understand. I'm s'posed to wait for somethin' to drop dead before I eat it. It's my job. That's just the way *le Bon Dieu* made me."

"*Le Bon Dieu?* Aw, *non!* Don't waste your breath talkin' 'bout the Good God," says Chicken Hawk. "Besides, *mon ami,* even if there is a God, what makes you think he cares whether you get your supper? You gotta do like me, look out fo' yourself. Here, let ol' Chicken Hawk show you how to do that thang."

With that, Mangeur de Poulet leaped into the air and started wildly flapping about in daring loop-the-loops and crazy figure eights, showing off like you've never seen. All of a sudden, he spied a juicy little rabbit right down there next to Buzzard's fence post.

"Aw, this'll show Buzzard," he thought. Chicken Hawk took dead aim and down he zoomed after that rabbit, faster and faster. But Rabbit was smart-smart. She saw Chicken Hawk's shadow closing in on her, and she jumped down her hole just as the big show-off came zooming in. By this time, Chicken Hawk was speeding so fast that his brakes couldn't save him and he slammed smack dab into that fence post! And down he dropped— thunk!—deader than the post itself, right at Buzzard's feet.

Buzzard looked down at that dead chicken hawk. Then he looked up to heaven. He grins real big and says, "*Merci beaucoup, mon Grand Bon Dieu!* Good God Almighty, thank you!" Then he jumps down off the fence post, smacks his lips, and says, "Suppertime!"

The Theft of Honey

Most Cajun people love to tell jokes and play pranks. If the joke backfires, so much the better; the trickster usually laughs harder than anyone else. It's no surprise that these trickster tales have traditionally been among Cajun people's favorite stories. This tale is African in origin but universal in its humor and insight.

Lapin was the smartest critter in all of Louisiana. That rabbit was such a smooth talkin' rascal that he could charm the whiskers off a cat and sell bacon to a pig. Lapin was full of trouble for true, and he just loved to play his tricks on all the other animals, especially his neighbor, Bouqui.

Now, Bouqui was a sneaky, skinny ol' fox, nervy as a gnat and all the time worrying and whining. Bouqui had plenty, but he was just plain greedy. He wouldn't share nothin' with nobody noway. But if he thought somebody else was getting more than him—ooowheee! How he'd moan and groan!

One day it happened that Bouqui and Lapin were walking together to the sugar cane field. Lapin took along some cornbread and cane *sirop* to eat for his dinner. Bouqui brought some fine light biscuits and a big jug of honey. Pretty soon, Bouqui starts bragging about his honey.

"Poor Lapin," he says, "all you gonna have for dinner is some ol' cane *sirop* and cornbread. But me, I'm gonna eat like a king. Just look at this big ol' jug o' sweet golden honey. It sure is gonna taste good!"

Lapin looks at Bouqui with a little twinkle in his eyes. "Well," he says, "why don't you just share some o' that good honey with your ol' friend, Lapin?"

Bouqui starts fussin'. "What you talkin' about, Lapin? No! I'm not gonna share with you. I brought this honey. If you want some, go get your own jug. This is my honey and you are not gonna get one little bitty drop!"

Lapin just grins real big and says to himself, "We'll just see 'bout that, *mon padnat.*"

Before they came to the cane field, Bouqui stopped and set his honey jug on the ground under a great big live oak tree. "There now," says Bouqui, "my honey'll keep nice and cool here in the shade—it'll be outta sight and outta mind. Lapin, you just forget about gettin' any o' this honey, you hear?"

Well, Lapin didn't say a word. He just went off to the field, whistling as he walked. They worked a spell in the rows of cane under the hot-hot sun. After a while Lapin started thinking about that sweet honey. His stomach got to growling, begging for just one little taste. Suddenly Lapin had an idea. He bolted right up, his ears searching the air and his nose just a twitchin'.

"Bouqui!" he hollers. "Do you hear? My wife is callin' me home. I have a new godchild!"

Bouqui hollers back, "I didn't hear nothin'!"

"Of course not, *mon ami,* your ears are too short. But my long ears hear my wife callin', 'Lapin! Come home quick!' So I gotta run home and help name the new *bébé.*"

With that, Lapin dashed across the field towards his house. But no sooner was he out of sight than he quietly circled back to the live oak tree. He picks up the jug of honey and gulp, gulp, gulp—a third of the honey is gone.

"Aaahhh! Bouqui was right," he says with a laugh. "This is good honey for true."

Lapin put the jug down, wiped his mouth, and returned to the field where Bouqui was still working.

"Hey, Lapin," yells Bouqui, "what did ya'll name the new *bébé?*"

Lapin grins and yells back, "An ol' family name. We gonna call that child Just Begun."

The two critters worked on in the heat of that hot, dry day. After a while, Lapin's stomach started talking to him again, growling for some more honey. So that rabbit jumps up, his ears listening and his big feet thumping.

"What is it now?" hollers Bouqui.

Lapin hollers back, "Do you not hear the news? My wife is callin' me, 'Come home, Lapin, you have another godchild!' I am a *parrain.* I must do my duty and help name the *bébé.*"

Before Bouqui could complain that he hadn't heard a thing, Lapin was bounding from the field towards his house. Once again he secretly circled back to the oak tree. Lapin picks up the jug of honey and gulp, gulp, gulp—the jug is half-empty.

"Oohwhee! I do believe this honey tastes better the second time around!" That rascal rabbit smacked his lips and snuck back to the cane field.

Bouqui yells out, "What ya'll gonna name this *bébé?*" Lapin chuckles and yells back, "Another ol' family name. We're gonna call this child Half-Done."

Lapin went back to work, but before long his stomach was pleading for just one more taste of honey. He jumps up, all ears and twitching nose.

He hollers out, "Bouqui! It's a miracle. I hear my wife callin' me, 'Lapin! Come home quick! You have another godchild!' I must run home quick-quick and help name the *bébé!*"

Bouqui listened and hollered back, "I don't hear nothin'!"

But Lapin was already racing across the field towards his house. Again he slyly circled back to the oak tree. He picks up the jug of honey and—gulp, gulp, gulp—the jug is empty.

"Aaahhh!" sighs Lapin. "Bouqui was surely right. I didn't get one little bitty drop—I got the whole jug." Then Lapin turned the empty jug upside down and set it back on the dry ground. He went back to the field feeling full and satisfied.

Bouqui shouts, "What ya'll gonna call this godchild?"

Lapin shakes with laughter and shouts back, "Oohwhee! We gonna call this *bébé* another ol' family name—All Gone."

Well, Bouqui and Lapin worked on a while longer till the sun was high in the sky and it was time to eat.

Bouqui hollers, "Dinnertime! I am so hungry! Man, that honey is sure gonna taste good."

The two critters walked across the field to the oak tree. When Bouqui found his honey jug turned upside down and empty, he started twitchin' and whinin'.

"My honey. It's all gone. Somebody ate all my honey! Somebody—Lapin! It must be you!"

But Lapin only looked hurt and surprised. *"Mon ami,* how can you say such a thing?" he asks. "Did you see me near your honey? Didn't you see me run to my house? Ah, my friend, surely you who are so much smarter than me can see what has happened. Just look at that jug turned upside down and empty on that hot, dry-dry ground. Just look how the ground is so dry and cracked and thirsty."

"What?" asks Bouqui in astonishment. "You mean the ground drank all my honey? Yes, I see it now. The ground stole my honey! Ooohhh!"

"Ah, *mon ami,*" says Lapin, nodding his head, "you have figured it out. You are so smart-smart! Poor Bouqui, now you have nothin' to eat with your biscuits. I tell you what I'm gonna do. I will share my *sirop* with you, and you can share your biscuits with me, eh? And maybe next time you have some honey, you'll share a few drops with your good friend, Lapin. After all, that's what friends are for, hmmm?"

Bouqui gladly took Lapin up on his offer. After they ate their dinner, they both stretched out in the shade and took a nap. Bouqui twitched and trembled in his sleep, but Lapin slept like a *bébé* and had sweet dreams—sweet as honey.

Fairy Tales

Catafo and the Devil

While my father, "Pa-Pa," was recuperating from surgery in an intensive care unit, I passed the long hours visiting with people in the waiting room. Being a storyteller in such an environment had its advantages. As people watched their loved ones struggle between life and death, they were eager to hear and tell stories that symbolized that battle for them. Mrs. Domingue, a woman of Cajun and Spanish stock, was one of the people who shared this story and others with me. Pa-Pa survived the ordeal. Later he told about a dream he'd had during his illness in which he, like Catafo, was forced to win his life back from the devil. He said ol' Devil screamed and hollered, "You cheated, you cheated!" In stories, as in life, ol' M'su Diable sure doesn't like it when somebody beats him at his own game!

Catafo and his two little brothers lived with their *maman* and *papa* in a cabin near the great woods. They were a poor family. They never had enough to eat, and they could not afford to move away in order to try to better their lives. Worry and hunger hardened the parents' hearts against the boys. One night when the children had gone to bed, Maman says, "We can't feed these boys anymore. There isn't enough food even for us. We gotta get rid of them."

"But how can we get rid of them?" asks Papa. "I don't have the heart to kill them."

"Tomorrow take them deep into the woods," she says. "When you're sure they're good and lost, leave them. Since we can't feed them, we'll leave them in God's hands. Live or die—it is up to Him."

The oldest brother, Catafo, heard every word. When his parents were asleep, he got up from bed, crept soft as a cat along the board floor, and filled his pockets full of flour. Early the next morning, sure enough, Papa woke the three boys up.

"Get up, sleepyheads," he calls. "Come walk with me in the woods."

The boys followed their *papa* out to the woods. As they walked along, Catafo sprinkled flour on the ground, marking their trail. On and on they walked until Papa figured the boys were hopelessly lost.

"Wait here for me," he says. "I'll be back in a little while to get you."

Papa disappeared in the deep, dark woods. The boys waited and waited, but Catafo knew Papa wasn't coming back. The little brothers were afraid and started crying. "Don't cry," says Catafo. "We're not really lost. See, I marked our trail with flour. Our parents don't want to feed us, and they thought they'd lose us in the woods. But all we have to do is follow the trail of flour back home."

The three boys found their way back home, arriving at the house just a little behind Papa. Maman was astonished to see them. That night after the children were in bed, Catafo overheard his parents plotting again to get rid of him and his brothers.

"Take them deeper into the woods tomorrow," says Maman. "Ol' man, this time you better be sure they're lost before you come back home, or maybe I'll have to get rid of you, too!"

When the parents had finally gone off to bed and were asleep, Catafo snuck out of bed and filled his pockets full of corn meal. The next morning Papa woke the boys at dawn. "Hurry and get up," he says. "You're goin' out to the woods with me!" He led the three boys farther and farther into the woods. He thought they would surely be lost this time, but he didn't notice that Catafo was marking their trail with corn meal. When they had walked far enough, Papa says, "Wait here for me. I'll be back before long. Stay right here. Don't try to follow me!"

The boys waited and waited. Papa never returned. The little brothers were hungry and frightened, and they began to sob. "Don't ya'll worry," Catafo says. "I left a trail of corn meal. We can get back home!" The boys started walking, but after about a half-mile or so, the trail of corn meal ran out. "A bird must've ate the corn meal up!" Catafo cried. The boys didn't have a clue how to get home. They were truly lost.

Catafo decided there was nothing to do but keep walking, although the little ones were afraid of the woods and didn't want to go any farther. "We can't just stay here or we'll starve," explains Catafo. "Be brave. I'll take care of you." When darkness came the boys refused to walk any farther. "Come on, just a little bit more; you never know what's up ahead!" Catafo says.

A few more steps and the boys saw a light shining through the woods. They tip-toed up and saw it was a house. Catafo knocked on the door. An old woman poked her head out. She was surprised to find three little boys all alone at her door so late. "Whata ya want?" she asks.

"Me and my brothers, we're lost in the woods. We been walkin' all day. We're so tired and hungry. Can you give us a place to sleep and a little supper? We won't be any trouble."

The ol' woman felt bad for the boys, but she shook her head. "My ol' man is a pure devil. If he comes back and catches you, he'll gobble you down whole!"

"Just let us sleep anywhere and give us a bite of food. He'll never know we're here," Catafo says.

The old woman took pity on the boys. She gave them a good supper and put them down on a little bed with a red quilt. Her own three devil-children were in another bed beside them, asleep under a blue quilt. Before long her he-devil husband came stomping home. Catafo woke up and heard him snortin' and sniffin' at the door.

"Hmm," that devil says, "I smell fresh meat!"

"It's just the beef I killed yesterday," the old woman tells him.

"No, it smells too good to be that kind of meat. I smell the sweet, tender meat of little boys, and I mean to eat them. You better tell me where you're hidin' them, or else!"

"Ol' man *diable,* I see I can't stop you from eatin' those poor lost children. Oh, that I should have such a devil of a husband, and three little devils for children! The boys you're looking for are sleeping under the red quilt. Your own little devil-brats sleep under the blue quilt. Take care that you don't get it mixed up!"

The he-devil went off and got his pots to boiling. He sharpened his axe. He was going to make an end of Catafo and his brothers, and cook them for his supper!

Catafo quickly woke his little bothers. "Shhhh! Get up. We've got to run for it!" Quick as a wink he fluffed up their moss pillows to look like three sleeping children. Then he switched quilts. He put the red quilt on the devil-children and the blue quilt over the pillows. The boys jumped out the window and ran for the woods.

The he-devil crept into the room with his sharp, shining axe. He peered at the quilts; his eyesight wasn't all that good anymore. He spied the bed with the red quilt. Three little shapes were snoring under the cover. Devil raised his axe, and chop, chop, chop! He killed his own devil children! When he pulled back the quilt and saw what he'd done, he flew into a rage. He flung off the blue quilt and saw he'd been tricked.

That ol' devil-man got on his big mule and took off looking for Catafo and his brothers. Before long the middle brother saw him coming. Catafo saw they were trapped.

"Quick! *Vite-vite!* Climb up this tree!" he says. "Do what I tell ya!" The three brothers scrambled up the tree. The he-devil rides up on his mule and sees the boys in the tree.

"Ha!" he says, "look what I've found. It's a boy-tree. Won't you look at those juicy little boys just waiting to drop like ripe figs! And looky here what I've brought: my magic bag. I've gotcha now—all you have to do is look down and you'll fall right inside my sack!"

The ol' devil-man spread his bag out under the tree. "Don't look down!" Catafo tells his brothers. "Look up at heaven instead!" All the little boys looked up at the moon and stars. The ol' man saw after a while it was no use, the boys wouldn't look down at his bag. So that *diable* lights a fire. He starts singing and dancing wildly around the flames. It's getting hard for the little boys not to look down.

"Don't look!" Catafo says, but it's too late. The youngest brother can't resist. He looks down, and shoom! He falls right into the bag, and it swallows him up.

Catafo and his middle brother could hear the terrified littlest boy crying inside the bag. Ol' he-devil is dancing faster now, singing and chanting. Suddenly the middle brother looks down. He falls, shoom! The magic sack swallows him up. Catafo could hear his poor little brothers crying for him, but he refused to look down. No matter how he sang and danced, the devil couldn't get Catafo to look down. "If you won't come down, then I'll just have to come up and getcha!" the devil shouts.

"Come on then," says Catafo. "Get me if you can." Catafo climbs to the highest branch. The devil climbs up just behind him. Suddenly, the boy shuts his eyes and jumps clear to the ground, landing on his feet like a cat! Catafo quickly frees his brothers from the bag. He laughs at the he-devil and says, "Look, M'su Diable, we have your magic bag. Look, we're getting away!" This made ol' devil so mad, he forgot his own magic and he looked down. All of a sudden, shoom! The devil falls kickin' and cussin' into the sack. It swallows him up with a big burp.

The little boys each got a big stick and beat the devil till he was flat as a pancake.

Catafo led his brothers back to the old woman. "We've killed your husband," Catafo says. "He won't bother anybody again."

The woman told the boys her husband had killed his own devil-children. "I'm glad to be rid of that mean ol' devil-man! His children were bad little devils, took after their bad ol' daddy. But still, I'm gonna miss them. Now I have no children."

Then the old woman thinks a moment and says, "You boys don't have anybody who wants you. Stay with me. I'll take care of you. You can be my sons."

So Catafo and his brothers stayed with the old woman. For the rest of their lives, they were satisfied and content.

King Peacock

I heard this tale from my grandmother when I was very young. My guess is that it came down to her from her maternal grandmother who came from France. I used to imagine the red seed of the magnolia cone as the magic red seed in the story—though it certainly must have been much smaller! Out behind our house was a pasture that turned into live oak woods. Within those great woods were an abandoned barn and a water tank. As a child, I thought that this was where the monster—the ogre of this story— lived.

There was once a lady who was the most beautiful woman in the world. On the outside she was all smooth skin and lovely eyes. But on the inside she was cold as winter. She couldn't love anyone but herself. She scorned all her suitors, saying, "You're not rich enough for my beauty" or "You are too ugly to marry me." In short, no man was good enough for her.

One day a fine-looking man came in a golden carriage. He was in love with the lady and asked her to marry him. But she refused, saying, "Ha! You want to marry me? You're not fit to wipe my boots!" The stranger's face twisted with rage and he set a curse on her: "In one year you will be delivered of a daughter who will grow to be more beautiful than you. She will become the most beautiful woman in the world. Then people will laugh behind your back at your foolishness!" But the lady only laughed at his curse and sent him away.

After some months, it became apparent that the lady was with child. She was filled with hatred, and she swore that if the baby was a girl she'd lock it away. Months passed and the child was born, a pretty baby girl. The lady did not even give her child a name. But the *bébé* was such a dear, so *chère,* that the child's nurse called the little girl Chérie.

For a long time the mother took no notice of Chérie, and each year the girl grew more and more beautiful. One day the lady saw that her daughter's beauty was greater than her own. She could not bear to look at her. She ordered Nurse, the old woman who cared for the child, to lock the girl away.

Chérie was put in a little room, and she was not allowed to leave or even look out the window. Years passed and the girl turned into a young woman. In all that time Nurse was her only friend, and Chérie was often lonely.

One day Nurse was sweeping the floor and, as she had left the door open, Chérie looked outside and saw, to her delight, a beautiful large bird with a tail of shimmering plumes.

"Nurse," she says, "what do you call that pretty creature?"

"That's a peacock, my child," says Nurse. "He is the king of the birds."

"Ah, Nurse," sighs Chérie, "If I ever leave this room and marry, I hope my husband will be as handsome as King Peacock!"

Nurse felt sorry for the girl. "May *le Bon Dieu* hear your prayers," she says.

The mother seldom visited her daughter, for she couldn't stand the sight of the girl's radiant face. Chérie's beauty haunted her until she thought she'd go mad. "I must put an end to her," she thought. "But how?" Each night she stood before her mirror plotting and planning. "When she's dead," she thinks, "no one will be prettier than me!"

One day the lady called Nurse to come and see her. She pulled a large, sharp knife out from under her petticoats. "I want you to kill my daughter!" she hisses. "She is more beautiful than me. I can not, I will not have it! Follow my orders or you can follow your precious Chérie straight to the grave yourself."

Nurse begged and pleaded but it was no use. The lady's heart was cold as ice. That night, Nurse told the girl that her mother had ordered her death. "But I do not have the heart to do it. Let us die together then, for I am sure there's no way to stop her from this evil deed."

But Chérie loved Nurse as a child loves its *maman*. "No," she pleads, "I won't let you die for me—you're my only friend. I'll take my own life, then you will live. There's no other way. I beg of you, do as I wish, for if you die on my account I will never rest in peace!"

Tears streamed down the old woman's face. "I will follow your wish though it breaks my heart, but I'll ease the way for you, *ma p'tite* Chérie. Here are three magic red seeds. Swallow one of them, then throw yourself down a well. You will feel no pain at all."

Chérie kissed Nurse and set out to drown herself in a well. She walked until she came to a wide well built of stones. She placed a seed in her mouth and jumped into the well. When she splashed into the water, the seed fell from her mouth and the water dried up, all in an instant. There she sat, unhurt, at the bottom of the well. Chérie was sorry to see the water had all dried up. "I'll just have to find another way," she thinks. The girl grasped the stones jutting out from the sides and climbed out of the well. She started walking and thinking of some other way to carry out her mother's command that she die.

Chérie walked a long-long way. Near suppertime she came to a cabin on the bank of a bayou. She knocked at the door and a woman old as Time itself answered. Her hair hung like moss and her hands were as gnarled as *boscoyo*. When the old woman saw Chérie she felt sorry for her. It was plain to see the girl was in desperate trouble. Why else would a pretty one like her be roaming a dark bayou? She squinted at the girl through her ancient eyes.

"Whatcha want? Whatcha doin' way out here, girl? Have ya lost your mind? Gone moon-mad? Don'tcha know my ol' man is an ogre? If he sees you he'll eat you up, for true!"

Chérie cries, "That is what I want! Maman wants to get rid of me. If I don't die she'll kill Nurse for not carrying out her orders. I can't bear the thought of poor ol' Nurse dying for me. I must end my own life to save hers. Oh, I have to die. What else is there to do?"

The old one understood such matters. After all, she was the oldest living thing around, and Time had made her wise.

"Follow your heart," she says, "and you'll find the answer. I've lived a long-long time, *p' tite fille,* and me, I know one thing for true, your death isn't gonna satisfy your *maman.* One of these days she's gonna find out her real enemy is Time." The old woman sighs and looks at her wrinkled, bony hands. "I used to be beautiful like you, now I'm a withered old thing. Ah, but no matter, I lost beauty but I got wisdom. Time took my beauty, but I didn't let it touch my heart! How do you think I got to be so old, eh?"

Just then they heard big, heavy footsteps coming. Thud, thud, thud! An ugly green ogre with big yellow teeth came into the room. He wrinkles his snout and sniffs loudly. "Grrrr," he growls, "I smell fresh meat. And there she is!"

He made ready to pounce on the girl and rip her to shreds, but the girl showed no fear. Her large, dark eyes were filled only with sorrow. Ogre was curious. Why didn't this girl act like a proper human, screamin' and beggin' for mercy?

"Aren't you scared I'll eat you up?" he asks. "Don't my ugly looks terrify you?"

"No, Ogre," says the girl with a sad smile. "I'm not afraid of your looks. You are not so ugly. Beauty that hides a wicked heart is uglier than you. My own mother is the most beautiful woman in the land, yet her heart is full of hatred and murder for me. Go ahead and eat me; you'll save me the trouble of ending my own life."

For the first time in his life, a human did not scream with horror at the sight of Ogre. He sadly nodded his head. "What you say is true," he says. "People say I'm bad just because I am so ugly. But can I help that? Their flesh is sweet to me only because I want revenge for their unjust curses. Yet I won't eat you, girl. Your face is pretty, but there are lots of pretty faces. It's your kindness that makes you beautiful, for true. Pass the night with us. You're tired and it's late. Don't be afraid of me. I won't touch a hair on your head. I'll only watch over you."

Before she lay down, Chérie put a red seed in her mouth. Better to end her life now and be done with it. The ogre might change his mind when he got hungry and eat her for breakfast. The old woman fanned her with a peacock feather and the girl drifted off into a deep-deep sleep. For three days she slept with no breath, her heart fluttering as softly as butterfly wings. When the girl failed to wake after three days, Ogre thought she must be dead. He cried as he gently laid her in a shining golden coffin. Ogre couldn't stand to bury her, for she was too beautiful. So he carried the coffin down to the bayou and put it into the water. With a little push, he sent the girl and the coffin floating downstream.

The coffin floated for three days until it passed into a faraway land. On the third day it happened that the king was walking on the *levée* with his counselors. Suddenly, he saw something shining like gold floating in the water. He ordered his counselors to fetch the thing. They went out in a little skiff and brought it back.

A gold coffin! The king had never seen anything like it and he was naturally very curious. "Some great king has died," he thinks. "I must look inside." He opened the lid and saw the girl. "This is a coffin for a queen, not a king!" He looked at the beautiful Chérie and was struck by love. She seemed somehow so fresh, so alive. Perhaps she was enchanted and he could find a way to wake her! He'd heard tell of such things happening.

He commanded his counselors to bring the coffin to the palace, where they laid the sleeping girl on a soft bed. The king rubbed her wrists and cheeks with rose water, but still the young woman did not open her eyes. He made loud, sharp sounds, thinking she'd be frightened out of her sleep, but she lay as unmoving as a statue. At last he believed she was dead. He couldn't let her go without one kiss, and he kneeled down beside her. But before his lips touched her lips, his moustache tickled her nose. A smile passed over her lips, and he saw something small and red caught between her pearly teeth. With a golden pin, the king removed the little seed.

At once, the young woman stretched and yawned. Her eyes fluttered open to behold a handsome man in shimmering clothing. "I must still be dreaming," she says, "for I was dreaming of a king, just like you, shimmering like a peacock!"

"Your dream has come true," the king said. "I am King Peacock. How strange it is—I've dreamed of a queen like you, too, a woman who will be dearer to me than my own life."

"Then you have dreamed true. My name is Chérie."

The couple were married and they returned to Chérie's home to free old Nurse. But in the meantime Chérie's mother had shriveled up with meanness and died from regret when she discovered that time always defeats beauty. Old Nurse rejoiced to see her *p'tite* Chérie again.

They brought Nurse back to the palace, where she lived out her days in peace. The king and queen lived for a hundred years. Time took their beauty, but their hearts stayed young. Beauty comes, beauty goes, but true love never grows old.

Baptiste and the Pirates

*Mrs. Domingue also related a fragment of this story. Later on I was able to find the other pieces. As always, the interpretation of the tale is my own. The character of Maman was very shadowy in all versions that I heard or found; but I thought of my **maman** and of my own little boy and girl, and I could well imagine Maman's heroic struggle to save her children in the hurricane-whipped seas. The story of a man overcoming one tragedy after another is classic.*

B aptiste owned a farm not far from La Ville. Unlike his rich neighbors he was not a man of wealth, but he was determined to turn the place into a great plantation. He worked hard and took extra care with his land until he was rewarded at last with a bountiful harvest. Cotton and sugar cane grew thick as hair, and his fields overflowed with potatoes, onions, and corn. At market he was a clever trader and his crops brought a high price. When Baptiste returned home he was a rich man.

To celebrate his good fortune after so many years of hard work, Baptiste decided to take his family on a trip to the old country. His wife was content to make the long journey, and their children, Jean and Marie, who had never been beyond Louisiana, were eager to see the wide-wide world.

Baptiste and his family sailed on a French ship loaded with bales of cotton. The first three days were uneventful. But on the fourth day a terrible hurricane fell upon them. The ship trembled and tossed like a cork upon the waves. Its timbers groaned, straining against the churning winds, but the boat was sturdy and held fast. At last, however, a giant wave crashed the ship into a jutting rock, and the sea threatened to claim her prize.

Maman saw she must take action or they would all soon drown. She quickly shoved a cotton bale into the water, told the children to hold on to her with all their might, and edged her way off the nearly sunken ship into the foaming water. She fought the ocean with a mother's desperate determination to save the lives of her children, even if it meant losing her own. At last she reached the floating cotton bale. The children climbed up on it and clung to the cords that bound it together. Maman was exhausted by her swim and barely able to drag her numb body onto the cotton bale.

Baptiste was nowhere to be seen. Maman and the children cried out for him again and again, but there was no answer. They feared he had drowned and they would never see him again. The little family wept. Their salty tears fell into the pounding sea as the wind swept the cotton bale far from the sunken ship into the dark-dark night.

They floated until morning, when the bale of cotton was washed up on an island. Maman led the children onto land and into a deep forest where they took shelter inside the hollow trunk of a great tree. They had not rested long, however, when Trouble and his sister, Sadness, came upon them.

Their first day on the island, Maman fell sick. She grew weaker and weaker until on the fourth day she died. Jean and Marie were lost without her. They could neither move from the cold, pale body of their mother nor cease their crying for her. At last, the horrible smell of death drove the children away from the body. Jean and Marie wandered the island, eating wild fruits and drinking from a little spring that flowed in the woods.

The children lived for many days without shelter or warmth. But as the months and years rolled by, they learned the art of survival and adapted themselves to the wild like the other creatures on the island.

One day, after three long years of waiting and watching, Jean and Marie spied a ship on the horizon. The children shouted and waved as it sailed closer and closer. The ship stopped, and to their great joy, Jean and Marie were carried on board. They were happy to be rescued and to taste good food again, and they believed that their trial was over at last.

Little did the children suspect the awful truth that they had been picked up by a band of wicked, cannibal pirates who planned to kill them, cook them, and eat them! The ship had been at sea a long time, and the pirates were hungry for fresh, tender meat. On the second day the children were locked away by the captain in a little room.

Jean tried in vain to open the door; the window was sealed with iron bars. There appeared to be no chance of escape.

Three times a day an old man with a long beard brought food to the boy and girl. He was not like the other pirates, but was kind to the children and comforted them with quiet conversation. On one such occasion, Jean and Marie told him the sad tale of their lost *papa* and dead *maman*. Tears came to the old man's eyes and his hands trembled, for he was Baptiste, and before him were his children who he thought had drowned!

He spoke their names and told them his own story. He had nearly drowned in the hurricane. Just as he thought he had breathed his last, something brushed against him in the storm-tossed water. He grabbed it and climbed on top—it was a bale of cotton. He floated until he thought he would die of thirst, when he was rescued by a passing ship. But more misfortune befell him. Baptiste soon discovered that his rescuers were really pirates, and he was forced to slave for them. Jean and Marie had not recognized him, for all his troubles had made him look older than his years. The children fell into their dear father's arms and wept tears of joy and pain. They were thankful to be reunited, but they all grieved for dear Maman.

Jean and Marie begged Papa to free them from their prison. "Have courage, my little ones," he whispered. "When the time is right I will come for you. There are seven pirates, and they will kill us for true if we are caught! So first, I must plan our escape. I must find some way to trick them. There are too many pirates for me to fight alone."

Jean and Marie waited a long time for Papa to free them. They asked him again and again if the time was near for their escape.

"You must wait a little longer," warned Baptiste. "But the time is near when I will come for you!"

Weeks passed. At last the pirates admitted their intention to kill and eat the children the very next day. That night, Baptiste secretly built a small raft of kegs and tied a bag of food and a jug of water to it. He hid the raft under a sail and volunteered to take watch with another pirate. When the hour grew late and the other pirates fell asleep, Baptiste brought out two jugs of rum.

"Come and drink!" he tells his mate. "Warm your bones on a cold night."

Baptiste had brought two jugs—one filled with strong rum, the other with molasses and water.

Baptiste dares the pirate, "Let us see who can outdrink the other!" He gave the vagabond the jug of rum and kept the jug of molasses water for himself.

The two men began to drink, matching swig for swig. Before long the pirate was singing and swaying, while Baptiste only acted drunk, laughing and stumbling. After many drinks, Baptiste began to hiccup. "You win, my friend," he said, and pretended to pass out. The pirate kept on gulping from the jug of rum until his eyes crossed and he dropped into a drunken sleep.

When the pirate was snoring loud enough to wake the dead, Baptiste crept up to the prison window and broke through the iron bars. Quickly and softly, he led the children to the raft and lowered them down to the quiet sea. He shimmied down a rope and climbed on with them. As fast as he could, Baptiste paddled away from the ship.

By the time the pirates found that Baptiste and the children were gone, it was too late. The little family had escaped for good!

They drifted for three days until they landed on the island of Cuba. Baptiste and his children were penniless and nearly starved in a strange land. To survive, all of them worked like slaves in the sugar cane fields. After eight long, hard years, they had saved enough money to buy passage back to Louisiana.

When they arrived at their old home they were heartbroken, for their land lay in ruins. The neighbors were amazed to see them again. When they heard all that had happened to the little family, they were shamed by their own greed and wealth. They all came together to help Baptiste clear his land and plant a crop. Another eight years of hard work followed, but at last the land once again gave the family a bountiful harvest.

Baptiste never became the owner of a great plantation as he had wished. But to the end of his days his life was rich with the harvest of his honest work and the blessing of his children's love.

Julie and Julien

In the early 1970s, I worked at my first job as a nurse's aide in a nursing home. It was there I met Miss Rosella, a ninety-three-year-old blind lady. I was a shy teenager and wondered what we could possibly find to talk about together. I soon discovered all I had to do was listen— Miss Rosella would do the rest. Born in 1880, she offered me a priceless gift, a rare took into the life and imagination of the nineteenth century.

Julien loved to gamble more than any young man around. The riskier the bet, the higher the ante, the better he liked the game. He'd gamble on anything, and often he lost just about everything. But Julien had the gift of luck. Just when it looked like he was gonna lose his shirt, he'd suddenly have a lucky streak and win the pot!

Now one day, Julien was passing by a saloon when he heard the sound of cards being shuffled and slapped down on a table. That was music to his ears! He went inside rubbing his hands. (His palms were plumb itchin', a sure sign he was comin' into money.) There he saw a man sitting alone, shuffling cards fast as lightnin'. He was a giant of a man with a long, bushy, blue beard hanging clear down to his knees. He was so ugly that Julien just stared at him.

The giant glared back at Julien. Suddenly, he pounds the table with a huge fist and growls, "Boy, you wanna play? Think you're good enough to beat ol' Blue Beard? I'm the best that is. You beat me, that makes you the best. But I gotta warn ya, son, the stakes are high. You best not play if you can't pay!"

Julien studied Blue Beard. The giant was strong enough to crush him in one blow. But the young man figured the giant wasn't too quick when it came to smarts. "Muscles won't win the pot," he thinks, "but brains will!" So he agrees to play cards.

They start playing. The cards are flappin' and slappin' so fast Julien can't keep track of them. He tries every trick he knows but it's no use, Blue Beard wins every time. Pretty soon, Blue Beard has won everything the boy owns; there's nothing left but the shirt on his back.

Blue Beard slams his cards on the table and hollers, "I win! Now pay up."

"I don't have anything left but my shirt!" says Julien.

"Ha!" barks the giant. "Your shirt! It won't cover your losses, stupid boy. I told you the ante was high. You play, you pay! But tell ya what I'm gonna do. Me, I'm a good-hearted fella, I'm gonna let you work off your debt. I'm gonna give you three weeks to find my house. You come and work for me for one year. If you don't show up, I'm gonna find you and destroy you."

"Then you gotta tell me how to get to your house," says Julien.

"Ha! That's a good one. Stupid boy, can't you see the game's not over? 'Where is my house?' you ask. That's for me to know and you to find out!" Blue Beard gathered all his winnings and stomped away, hollering, "Three weeks. You better show up for work or else!"

Julien was worried. He was in a fix for true. He thought and thought, but he couldn't figure how he was gonna find out where the giant lived. At last an idea came to him. "My ol' *grandmaman* is smart-smart. I'll go see her and ask her where the giant lives."

Julien went to his *grandmaman* and told her all his troubles. The old lady shook her head and says, "I don't know the way to the giant's house, but maybe I know somebody who can help you. Tonight when the moon is full, go out to the river and walk along the bank. If you are lucky, you'll meet an old-old woman. Ask her where Blue Beard lives. She can talk in the wild way of all the creatures. Maybe one of the wild things knows how to get there."

Julien did as his *grandmaman* said. He walked along the river bank in the moonlight, calling out, "Old one! Old one!"

Just then, an ancient woman with long, flowing, silvery hair appeared. "Who calls me?" she asks.

"I am Julien," he says. "My *grandmaman* said you could help me. I have to find the house of Blue Beard, the giant, in three weeks or else he'll kill me! But nobody knows where he lives. Can you tell me the way?"

"I don't know," says the old one, "but I will call the creatures and ask them. Maybe they have passed by the house of Blue Beard."

She cried out in the voices of the wild things. Animals large and small gathered around them in the darkness. "Who can help this young man? He looks for Blue Beard. Who knows the way to the giant's house?"

All the creatures were silent. At last the eagle says, "I flew by there yesterday. It is a dark and fearful place. Nobody goes there! But now the moon is full. Follow me and I will lead you, Julien."

Julien was amazed, for he could understand eagle talk! All night he followed the great bird. Just before dawn, they stopped. "You will find the house of Blue Beard through that thicket," the eagle said. "Take care to hide from the giant's three daughters. They've never seen a man before and are sure to raise a ruckus and wake the giant in a foul mood. *Bonne chance, mon ami!* Good luck!"

The eagle flapped away and Julien started through the thicket. He reached the house a little past dawn. Trees and flowers grew up thick all about the place. He hid among the branches of a flowering bush, waiting for something to happen.

The sun was climbing high in the sky when three girls came into the yard and began picking flowers. Soon enough the youngest girl, whose name was Julie, found the young man hiding in the bush. "Sisters!" she calls out. "Come and see what I've found. It's some kind of man, but he's not at all like Papa. He's little!" The other girls were afraid and called their sister to come away from the bush. But Julie was bold; she would not leave the bush until the young man came out.

That evening when Blue Beard came home, he found Julien sitting on his *galerie*. The giant wasn't at all happy to see the young man. But the game wasn't over. Blue Beard still had a few tricks up his sleeve.

"So, you found my place," he bellows. "Tomorrow you begin work. We'll just see how smart you are then."

Next morning Blue Beard took Julien to the bayou. He handed the young man a leaky old basket and a thimble and says, "Empty all the water outta this arm of the sea before supper, or I'll kill you!"

The giant went away and Julien was so scared he sat on the bank and cried. But the giant's youngest daughter, Julie, had followed them. She steps up and says, "Don't cry. I can help you. I have a few tricks of my own! Here's what to do: Take this little wand and wave it over the water at four o'clock. Say, 'By the virtue of this wand, may this arm of the sea be dry when Blue Beard gets here.' Then go and fill the thimble with the last drops of water and throw it at Papa's feet."

Julien did what Julie told him to do. He waved the wand and spoke the words. Sure enough, all the water disappeared except for three drops. He filled the thimble with the last three drops and tossed it before the giant's feet, saying, "Done is done!"

Blue Beard was mad enough to bust, but there was nothing he could do except try to trick Julien again the next day. In the morning, the giant took Julien to some thick woods. He handed the young man a wooden axe and says, "Chop all these trees down before supper. If you don't have this land cleared by then, I'll kill you!"

Blue Beard stomped off and Julien sat down, just about worried to death.

He began to cry. Suddenly, Julie appeared again by his side. She had fallen in love with him and could not bear to see him so worried. "Don't cry," she says. "I'll help you. Papa isn't the only one who can make magic. Do this: just before he returns, wish that the land be cleared with only one branch left. When Papa comes, grab that last branch and throw it on the pile. Everything will be all right, I guarantee!"

Julien followed her directions. He made the wish and shoom! The trees were all chopped down and piled high. He picked up the last little branch and threw it on the pile just as the giant came stompin' up. Julien dusted off his hands and says to the giant, "Done is done!" Blue Beard was so furious he stomped his feet and tore his beard. But all he could do was wait till the next day and try to trick Julien again.

That evening, Julie heard her *papa* whisper to Maman, "That Julien is too smart-smart. I believe I'll just make an end of him tomorrow. I'm tired of him beatin' me at my own game. Like I always say, if you can't beat 'em, then cheat 'em."

The giant's wife wasn't so sure that Julien was all that smart. Maybe he had help? "You watch that boy," she whispers, "and me, I'll watch our clever little daughter, Julie. It's plain to see she has fallen in love with that foolish young man."

Julie told Julien what she had heard. "Papa plans to kill you tomorrow! We have to escape. Tonight I'll put a charm on three beans. I'll leave them on the table on a plate. If Papa wakes up and calls us in the night, the beans will answer in our place. By the time he figures out we're gone, we'll have a big head start."

That night, Julie waited until Blue Beard and Maman were snoring, and then put the enhanted beans on the table.

Quiet as mice, Julie and Julien slipped out of the house and ran away into the moonlit night. In the middle of the night, Maman raised up and shook her husband awake. "Get up and go check on those two. I just know they're up to somethin'!"

Blue Beard was too sleepy to get out of bed, so he calls out, "Julie? Julien?"

The first bean on the plate answers in Julie's voice, *"Oui,* Papa. What do you want?"

"There," he says, "did you hear with your own ears? They are here." He rolled over and fell asleep.

But Maman tossed and turned. Once again she woke her husband. "Call them again. I just know they've run away!"

Blue Beard calls out again, "Julie? Julien?" The second bean on the plate answers, *"Oui,* Papa. What is it?"

"See?" growls Blue Beard, "I told you they're here. Now can I get some sleep?"

Pretty soon Blue Beard was snoring, but Maman still tossed and turned, certain something was wrong. "Call them again. Something is goin' on, I just know it!"

The giant hollers out, "Julie? Julien?" The third *fève* on the dish answers, *"Oui,* Papa. What do you want?"

"I told you they're here!" the giant roars. "Now leave me alone!"

But his wife suddenly figured out what was wrong. "Wait a minute. Why doesn't that foolish boy answer back?" She calls out, "Julie? Julien?" But this time there's no answer at all. "Get up," she shouts. "They've escaped! If you get started now you'll catch up with them by mornin'."

Blue Beard growled with fury at being roused out of bed in the middle of the night. He jumped astride his giant horse and galloped off to find the couple that had tricked him.

All night Julie and Julien traveled. At daybreak Julie warned Julien to be on the lookout for anything that seemed strange. "Papa is full of tricks. You can bet he's not through with you yet!"

Just then Julien saw something in the distance: a rider on a terrible horse coming in a cloud of smoke. "It's Papa!" Julie cries. "Quick, I'll turn us into two little pigs. Run into the stickers fast as you can."

A few magic words and shoom! Julie and Julien turned into two little pigs. They ran into the thicket just as Blue Beard rode up.

"Pigs?" he says. "Pigs in the middle of nowhere? Let's just have another look." Blue Beard ran into the stickers and tried to catch the pigs, but they were just too fast for the lumbering giant. The stickers caught and tore at his beard. At last Blue Beard gave up the chase. He got back on his horse and headed home.

Maman was waiting on the *galerie*. "Well, did you see them?" she asks.

"Nothin' but some little pigs runnin' like greased lightnin' through a thorny thicket," he says.

"You idiot! Those pigs were Julie and Julien!" she hollers. "It's just like I thought. She's been helping that boy all along. Get back on your horse. Go catch them! They can't have gone far."

Blue Beard grumbled like thunder, but he got on his horse and rode off like a windstorm in search of his daughter and her young man.

In the meantime, Julie and Julien were traveling as fast as they could. "Let's stop and rest," Julien says. "Blue Beard has given up and turned back."

"Oh, you can bet he'll be back. Look, who's that comin'?" Sure enough, there was a distant rider coming in a cloud of smoke. "It's Papa!" she hisses. "Quick, I'll turn us into rose bushes. Now sit still. Don't move a muscle."

A few magic words and shoom! They turned into a couple of red rose bushes. Blue Beard came ridin' up, but nothing but flower bushes was to be seen. Didn't it seem like one of the bushes was moving? The giant reached out to pick a rose, but the thorns pricked him so he gave it up. He was tired of all this chasin' around. He climbed on his tired horse and crept back home.

His wife was pacing up and down the *galerie*. "Well, did you see anything, any sign of them?"

"Just a couple of rose bushes that stuck me when I tried to pick their flowers," says the giant.

"What an idiot!" she cries. "Those roses were Julie and Julien. Give me that horse. This time I'll go!" Blue Beard's wife jumped on the horse and galloped away to find the young couple.

By this time, Julie and Julien had come to a river. But in the distance they once again spied a rider coming up on them. "It is Maman," says Julie, "and she won't be so easy to trick. I'll change us into ducks. Whatever you do, stay close to me."

A few magic words and shoom! The couple turned into two ducks. They jumped into the river and paddled off.

Maman rode up to the bank and began to call out to the ducks. The male would swim towards her, but each time the little female would head him off. At last Maman threw up her hands. "You win!" she hollers. "We won't bother ya'll again. You have won your freedom." Maman turned back to tell Blue Beard the bad news: he had lost the game.

The two ducks swam to an island and waddled up the beach. At once they were changed back into Julie and Julien. They were very happy to be free at last. Together they made themselves a little house and were content with what the island could provide them.

They continued in their happiness for many months until one day Julien complained to Julie that he was homesick. "I haven't seen my family for so long. They must think I'm dead. I have to go show them I'm alive and well. I won't be gone all that long!"

"If you leave, you'll forget me!" Julie cries.

"How could I forget you, *chère?* Never!"

"All right then," Julie says, "go and see your family. But promise me one thing: you won't let anybody kiss you."

Julien thought it was a strange promise, but he did as she asked and set out on his journey. He walked and walked until he reached his old home. His family was overjoyed to see him and they wanted to kiss him. But Julien only pushed them away. "I am married to the smartest girl you ever saw, and she says I will forget all about her if you kiss me. I made her a promise that nobody would kiss me!"

The family thought it was a strange promise too, but they agreed not to kiss him. That night, the young man's *maman* passed by as he lay in bed sleeping. She was so happy to have her boy home that she forgot all about the promise. She kissed him gently on his forehead.

When Julien woke up, he had forgotten everything. He couldn't remember having a wife called Julie at all. "You must have heard wrong. I have no wife, no wife at all," he insisted.

Months passed and the family gave up trying to wake Julien's memory. He began to court another lady, and before long the couple announced their wedding plans.

It was to be a large wedding. Cousins were invited from up and down the river for miles. At last the day of the wedding arrived, and Julien's third cousin once removed showed up with a mysterious guest, a widow woman in a dark veil.

She had promised to entertain all with the rooster and the little hen that she carried in her arms. Everyone was eager to see the show and they gathered around. Julien and the bride-to-be stood at the front of the crowd.

The widow put the rooster and the hen on the table, with a grain of corn between them. Suddenly, the rooster gobbled up the grain of corn and the hen began to talk. "Well," says the little hen, "aren't you somethin'? You don't remember anything I've done for you!"

"How's that?" asks the rooster. "What have you done for me?"

"Ah," says the hen, "I only saved your life three times. You left me with a promise that nobody would kiss you. Now just look—the promise is broken, and you have forgotten the one who loves you more than anyone!" With that, the hen pecked the little rooster on the head.

All of a sudden, Julien remembered everything. He threw back the widow's veil, and behold! It was Julie. "Ah, *ma chérie,* forgive me! How could I forget the best wife a man ever had?"

But then he remembered the occasion, his wedding. "Hmmm," he thinks, "but what to do about the other bride waiting to marry me?"

Julien went to the bride's father and asked him a riddle. "If you lost a key and bought a new one, and then, on the way home, found your old key again, what would you do with the new key?"

The man thought and answers, "Why, I'd take the new key back and keep the old key."

"Well," says Julien, "I've found my old memories and my wife, so I'm giving my new bride, your daughter, back to you."

Everyone rejoiced to see that Julien was his old self again. They were happy to see he'd married such a smart-smart woman as Julie. It took a while, but even the bride-to-be and her father forgave him. It was a lucky thing, too, for things could have gone hard for him. But then, Julien always was a very lucky young man indeed.

Jean Malin and the Bull-Man

*I come from a family that rates fishing as a near holy activity. When I brought my husband-to-be home to meet my parents, their first question was, "Do ya like to fish?" Like everyone in my family, I fish whenever and wherever I can. Once in Louisiana I saw some folks fishing in a bayou and I stopped to join them. I sat down by an elderly Creole lady and she started to talk. I didn't catch any fish that day, but I sure hooked some good stories from Miss Fontenot, my fishing partner. She told this story and a few others. She was known as a healer (**traiteur**) and shared some of her remedies (though not her special healing prayers, which always remain secret) with me.*

Jean Malin was the trickiest boy in Louisiana. He was some kind of smart-smart for true! It's a good thing, too, for Jean Malin was only a child when his parents passed. He was left alone in the wide-wide world to look after himself. At first the boy didn't know what to do. But Jean Malin wasn't only clever—he was also very lucky.

ng before the boy's curiosity brought him good

dy passed by in a fancy carriage. Jean had
g like it. He ran beside it, curious to
have a look. The lady saw the boy and admired his bright
eyes and clever manner. She halted the carriage and
inquired of the boy his name and age.

"They call me Jean Malin," says the boy. "I don't
know how old I am, but my poor *maman* told me I was
born in a year when snow fell and the peach trees
bloomed." When the lady heard that Jean Malin was all
alone, she asked him to come live with her.

"Well," says Jean Malin to himself, "I could do a lot
worse for a stepmother!" So he climbed into the carriage
and off they went to the lady's fine home.

Jean Malin worked as a servant in the fancy house.
He came to love his stepmother as his own *maman*. He
thought of himself as the man of the house and did his best
to look out for his *belle-mère*. She was kind and rich, easy
pickin's for a shrewd man with a greedy heart.

One day a handsome gentleman came to call. The man
was just nice as pie, but Jean Malin didn't trust him at all.
There was something suspicious about him. The boy kept
his eyes and ears open, waiting for the stranger to slip up
and show his true self.

Before long Jean Malin became aware of a great black
bull out on the prairie. Each evening the boy saw the bull,
but in the daytime it disappeared. He soon also observed
that the stranger came courting only when the bull was
gone. When the stranger left, the bull appeared once again.
Jean Malin decided to follow the stranger one day. The

boy was sly and trailed after the man like a silent shadow; the man had no idea the boy was behind him.

The stranger walks out into the prairie, looks all around, then bends down on his knees and sings:

> *Bonheur, Mamselle, bon, bon, bon!*
> *Bonheur, Mamselle! C'est bon, bon, bon!*

Quick as a wink, shoom! The man was changed into a big black bull.

Jean Malin couldn't believe his eyes. "Ah, so that is his secret!" the boy thinks. He snuck back home, taking care not to be seen by the bull. The next morning, he crept back to the prairie and hid himself, waiting to see what would happen. He watched the bull bend down and heard it sing:

> *Bonheur, Mamselle, bon, bon, bon!*
> *Bonheur, Mamselle! C'est bon, bon, bon!*

Boom! The bull changes back into the handsome gentleman. Jean Malin was afraid for Belle-Mère. The kind lady was in danger! The bull-man surely meant to marry Mamselle, kill her, and make off with her fortune!

The boy followed the stranger to his stepmother's house. "I've gotta warn her," he thinks, "before ol' Bull-Man tricks her into marriage." When he got to the house he found the bull-man sitting with his stepmother, eating breakfast. The boy commenced serving them, but he was so scared that he kept dropping things and confusing orders. When the lady asked for a fork, he gave her a plate, and he spilled or broke everything he touched.

When the gentleman left, Belle-Mere fussed at the boy. "What is the matter with you? Why don't you like my caller? You had better get used to him because I might just marry him. If you don't behave yourself, I'll send you away!"

Jean Malin was trembling with fear. "I will tell you, Mamselle, but I'm afraid," he says. "If you'd seen what I saw, you'd be afraid too. You'd never let that man in your house again."

The boy's stepmother was really mad now. "Tell me what you know at once. *Vite-vite!* Out with it, boy, before I whip you and hang you on the fence for *tasso!*"

"All right then," says Jean Malin, "here it is. Your caller is up to some evil trick. Each evenin' he says some magic words and changes into a big black bull. Then, in the morning, he says the words again and changes back into a man before he comes to court you. I swear it is the truth! I will prove it when he calls on you again. If I am lying, Mamselle, you can punish me any way you want or send me away forever."

"I think you are a mean, spiteful thing," says the lady, "just jealous of my gentleman. But I love you like my own son, so I'm gonna give you a chance to prove yourself."

The next day Bull-Man shows up in his handsome gentleman disguise. He sits down to dinner with Mamselle and flashes his charming smile. As the boy pours wine into their glasses, the gentleman asks Mamselle to marry him. But before she can say a word, Jean Malin shouts out the bull-man's magic words:

Bonheur, Mamselle, bon, bon, bon!
Bonheur, Mamselle! C'est bon, bon, bon!

And shoom! All of a sudden a bull is sitting at the table! The animal starts bellowing and kicking everything in sight, breaking the dishes and shattering the crystal. At last the mad bull smashes through the window and escapes.

Belle-Mère was grateful to her stepson. He had surely saved her life. Jean Malin and Mamselle thought they would have some peace at last, but soon the word reached them: M'su Taureau, the bull, had sworn revenge on Jean Malin. The bull wouldn't be satisfied until he had killed the boy.

One day Jean Malin met up with Lapin the rabbit. "M'su Lapin," says the boy, "they say you're the smartest critter around. I'm in big trouble with M'su Taureau. That mean ol' bull swears he's gonna kill me! Can you help me?"

Lapin just laughs and says, "Oohwhee, I can help you fix that ol' bull for good! He won't ever bother you no more. Here's whatcha gotta do. Today is Friday. Go into the woods and find Owl's nest. Wait till sunset and get three eggs, then bring them to me. I'm gonna lay such a *gris-gris* on'm that M'su Taureau will wish he never messed with you!"

Jean Malin got the eggs and Lapin put the charm on them. Then that rascal rabbit whispered into the boy's ear and told him how to use the eggs. *"Bonne chance, mon padnat!"* says Lapin. "You just tell M'su Taureau you got powerful friends like ol' Lapin!" That critter just cracked up laughing and jumped back down his rabbit hole.

Jean Malin hurried home. Sure enough, there was M'su Taureau, bellowing and kicking up dust. "Now I'm gonna kill you, boy," he snorts. "You think you're so smart. How you gonna save your scrawny neck this time? Huh?"

The bull charges at the boy, trying to gore him with those sharp horns, but Jean Malin is too fast. He scrambles up a tree like a squirrel and hangs on to the top branch.

Well, ol' Bull is so mad he's about to bust. He kneels down, sings his magic song, and shoom! He's a man. He gets an axe and starts chopping on the tree. Gip, gop, gip, gop! Bull-Man hollers, "You can't outsmart me this time, Jean Malin. I'm gonna chop you up just like I'm choppin' this tree down!"

All of a sudden, the boy pulls something out of his pocket. It's an owl egg. He takes aim and throws the magic egg at Bull-Man. The egg explodes against his shoulder. Boom! Bull-Man's right arm drops off.

Bull-Man starts chopping like crazy with his left arm. Gip, gop, gip, gop! But Jean Malin takes the second egg and sends it flying at him. The egg hits Bull-Man on the other shoulder. Boom! His left arm falls off. Bull-Man is so mad he picks up the axe in his teeth and starts chopping faster and faster. Gip, gop, gip, gop, gip, gop!

"Now to finish you off!" says Jean Malin. The boy takes the third egg and hurls it at Bull-Man. It hits Bull-Man right between the eyes. Boom! His head falls off.

Then Jean Malin starts singing the magic song:

> *Bonheur, Mamselle, bon, bon, bon!*
> *Bonheur, Mamselle! C'est bon, bon, bon!*

Right away, Bull-Man's arms and head go to wigglin' like worms on a hook. Shoom! The body parts turn into a bull again. "Now get on outta here," hollers Jean Malin, "before I do worse to ya!" The bull bellows with fear and off he gallops.

M'su Taureau the bull never did bother Mamselle or Jean Malin again. That boy was just too blame smart. And besides, ol' Bull-Man figured out that Jean Malin had powerful friends in low places—like rabbit holes!

Marie Jolie

*This is my all-time favorite story. I heard the skeleton of the tale from my grandmother. The interpretation is my own, however, a combination of personal experiences and the stories passed down by several generations of grandmothers and aunts. As a young woman I worked for an oil seismograph crew along stretches of the Mississippi River. Sometimes when the sun was just coming up on the **levée** and fog lay like a shroud over the water, I thought I could hear Marie in the distance calling ol' Grandmaman Alligator. Even though I knew it was only my imagination, I'd get a shiver down my spine, and I'd just have to look over my shoulder to make sure ol' M'su Diable wasn't behind me!*

Down in the bayou country there was once a beautiful girl named Marie. She was so pretty, so *jolie,* that all the people called her Marie Jolie. She was as sweet as sugar cane, but if you did her wrong, look out, for that girl could show a temper as hot as cayenne pepper!

Now Marie Jolie grew to be of a marrying age, but to her *maman's* disappointment, she wasn't yet of a mind to be married. First, she wanted to have adventures and see the big world, so she found something wrong with every young man who came to court her. This one was too short; that one was too tall; the next one had the ears of an elephant.

After a while her *maman* got impatient with Marie, for she worried that her daughter would wind up an old maid—a terrible fate in those days. So Maman says, "Marie Jolie, it is time for you to take a husband. You can't pick one to suit you, so me, I'm gonna do it for you. We gonna have us a contest. You see this pumpkin? I'm gonna get M'su Carencro, the buzzard, to put it on the highest little skinniest branch of that big cypress tree out there in the swamp. *Chère,* the man that can fetch that pumpkin down without fallin' in the water is gonna be your husband!"

"Well, Maman," says Marie, "if it's got to be, I s'pose that's as good a way as any of choosin' a man."

The contest was held the following week. Men came from parishes far and near, each one more eager than the next to win the hand of Marie Jolie. But one, a tall, dark, handsome man, stood out from the crowd. "Ooh, Maman," says Marie, "I hope he gets the pumpkin! He's a good-lookin' devil for true."

One after the other, the men tried to climb the great cypress, but they all ended up spitting swamp water. At last the good lookin' stranger's turn came. Quick as lightnin', he scaled that tree like a cat, snatched the pumpkin, and landed with his boots on dry land. Before she knew it, Marie Jolie was a married woman!

She climbed proud as could be into her husband's wagon, and they started driving down the road. It wasn't long, however, before she noticed that things were getting strange. The path was growing darker and darker, and her new husband uglier and uglier.

Suddenly, a fearsome man appeared beside the path. "Gimme my tie and collar which I lent ya!" he calls out. Marie's husband took off the tie and collar. "Here, then," he says, "take back your ol' tie and collar."

A little farther down the road, they met another man. He says, "Gimme back my coat which I lent ya!" "Take your ol' coat," says her husband.

Yet a third man appeared and demanded his trousers; a fourth demanded his hat. A little while later, her husband stopped the wagon, disappeared briefly into the swamp woods, and returned just as well dressed as before!

Finally, a fifth man, fiercer than all the others together, his face hidden in the shadow of his tall hat, appeared before them and pointed a long, bony finger. "Give me the horses which I lent ya!" he roars. "Go to the devil, then," says her husband with a wicked laugh, "and take your ol' horses with ya."

He watched as the man led the animals away, then he turned to his wife and hissed, "Girl, get down and hitch ya'self to the wagon and pull us home!" Marie Jolie could feel her temper rising. She was gonna tell him a thing or two! But a terrible change had come over her husband. His icy glare and ugly scowl frightened her. She thought she had better do as he said at least for a little while. She climbed down, hitched herself to the wagon, and began to pull with all her strength.

At last they arrived at her husband's *cabane*. It was a gloomy lookin' place, set way back in the swamp woods. "Marie Jolie," says her husband, "I must leave. While I am gone, you will stay here and see no one. My *maman* will take good care of you." And he disapeared in a burst of flames and smoke.

Marie was scared for true. She begged her new momma-in-law, "Please, Belle-Mère, tell me why my husband is so strange."

Belle-Mère, who was a kind woman at heart and felt worse than anybody about how her son had turned out, sadly shook her head. "Oh, *chère fille*," she says, "you've made a terrible match. You have gone and married M'su Diable, the devil himself!"

Marie couldn't believe her ears. "Old woman, you are only jealous. You just want to break up my marriage."

"You do not believe me, *p' tite fille?* Come with me," the old woman whispered. She led Marie Jolie inside the house to a secret door. She unlocked it with a big brass key and the heavy door creaked open. There, inside that dim room, Marie saw … the devil's other wives—each one hanging from a hook!

Now Marie Jolie knew the truth. "Oh, please, Belle-Mère," she cried, "you gotta tell me how I can escape! How can I get out of here?"

"Girl, do you not see what became of the others who tried to escape? Stay with me, little one, I will keep you company and ease your suffering," Belle-Mère pleaded. "Do not bring down the terrible wrath of my son, the devil!"

But Marie Jolie was growing angry, and in her anger she grew bold. "No," she insisted, "I will not be the devil's wife! If you won't help me escape, then I'll find a way on my own."

Belle-Mère sighed. "The devil knows many tricks. He can change into fire and smoke and ride the wind. You cannot outrun him, but maybe if you are brave enough you can outsmart him. Even the devil cannot defeat a strong heart. But if your courage fails, he will destroy you."

Marie was determined. "My heart is strong and my mind is made up," she said. "M'su Diable will not destroy me."

"All right then," says Belle-Mère, "here is what you must do. M'su Diable will return in the deepest night, at three o'clock, the soul's hour. He hates dawn and the rising sun. In its light he cannot hide his true self, so he sleeps. His spy, Gaime, the rooster, keeps watch. If he catches you tryin' to escape, he will crow. Tonight you must feed Gaime three bags of corn instead of one, so that he will oversleep. At sunrise, go and gather six dirty eggs. They will protect you. Do not take the clean eggs, for they are bad luck. Then, *chère,* run as quick-quick as you can away from this place!"

Marie did as she was told. Rooster overslept and she got the six dirty eggs. She tiptoed out, soft-soft, but the gate hinge squeaked and Gaime woke up crowin' full-throat. "M'su Diable, M'su Diable, wake up! *Vite-vite!* Your wife is gettin' away!"

Marie ran for her life as M'su Diable came screaming after her. She had not gone far when she turned and saw a cloud of smoke and fire approaching. She took one dirty egg and threw it over her shoulder. Boom! It exploded right in the devil's path, and a fence of wood as high and wide as the eye could see sprang up. M'su Diable snorted and stomped in fury and flew back to his *cabane*. When he returned, he had his magic golden axe. The axe chopped through the fence at once, and the devil was again hot on the trail of his runaway wife.

Marie grabbed a second dirty egg and heaved it straight at the devil. Crack! It flashed like a bolt of lightning, and a fence of brick sprang up as high and wide as the eye could see. The devil cursed and spat, and his magic axe smashed the brick to splinters.

Marie took aim and flung the third dirty egg. It shattered like thunder, and a fence of stone sprang up as high and wide as the eye could see. The devil shrieked and set his axe to ripping through the wall, and soon the cloud of fire and smoke again threatened to destroy her.

Marie took the fourth egg and hurled it through the air. The earth shook with its force, and a fence of iron sprang up as high and wide as the eye could see. But it too was little trouble for M'su Diable's fearsome magic.

Marie ran as fast as she could, but M'su Diable was almost upon her. She grabbed the fifth egg and pitched it straight into the fireball behind her. A wall of flames roared to the sky, and a deep bayou appeared before the devil. The water stopped him cold. But suddenly a great gust of wind blew the evil cloud of smoke and fire over the bayou, and the waters began to boil.

Marie's blood ran cold as ice when she looked back this time. For M'su Diable had dropped his disguise, and now she saw the ol' devil himself as he truly is. His forked tail whipped wildly about, his cloven hooves raised clouds of dust, and his goat beard flapped wickedly in the wind. The bright sun glinted off his sharp, curved horns, and his beady eyes burned like hot coals. Crusty red scales covered his body. For true, M'su Diable looked a whole lot like a boiled crawfish!

Only one dirty egg remained, and Marie threw it with her last ounce of strength. But her hand trembled so that she completely missed her mark. The egg fell at her own two feet and exploded. The earth rumbled and cracked. A mighty river came rolling by. It was the Mississippi! Marie was trapped. How could she ever swim such a wide, dangerous river?

But wait—wasn't that ol' Grandmaman Cocodrie sunning herself out there in the shallows? Marie cried out to the alligator, *"Je vous en prie, Grandmaman, traversez-moi. Sauvez ma vie! Aidez-moi, vieille Grandmaman!* I beg you, carry me across. Save my life. Help me, old Grandmother!"

Grandmaman Cocodrie, always on the lookout for an easy meal, swam up to Marie without a moment's hesitation. "Maybe I will carry you across," she growled. "But tell me, what makes you think I won't eat you up?"

"Grandmaman," says Marie, "I'd rather be your supper than be the devil's wife!"

"Climb on my back, *p'tite fille,* I like your courage!" says the old *cocodrie,* and she carried Marie quickly and safely to the other side.

Just then, M'su Diable came running up to the bank. In his most charming voice he called out, *"Traversez-moi, Grandmaman, traversez-moi! Belle, belle cocodrie!* Carry me across, old Grandmother, carry me across! Beautiful, beautiful alligator!"

"Climb on my back, M'su, I'll give you a ride for sure," says ol' Alligator with a snap of her jaws. M'su Diable stepped onto her scaly back, holding his forked tail out of the muddy water, while Grandmother Alligator swam out into the deep river.

Things were looking awfully bad for Marie, with M'su Diable closing in on her. But, if there was anything that Grandmaman Cocodrie hated, it was a mean ol' devil on her back, and suddenly, way out there where the water was swiftest and darkest, she dived. M'su Diable didn't have a snowball's chance in August. M'su Diable, of course, can't swim a lick—not much water down where he comes from. The Ol' Muddy took that devil kickin' and sputterin' all the way downstream to New Orleans. Some say he washed up in the French Quarter, right smack dab in the middle of Bourbon Street, but then, that's another story altogether.

As for Marie Jolie, she lived to be *une très vieille femme,* a very old woman. She had many adventures before her black hair turned snow-white. People called her Marie Esprit, the spirited one. When they asked why she never married again, she'd just smile and say, "You know, *chère,* once you been married to one devil, there's no need to go out and look for another one!"

The Magic Gifts

Mr. Laurence Molleré loved to tell this story about the "dancin' fiddle, the magic hat, and the shoot' em up gun." He especially liked the part where the boy gets the sheriff, the judge, and the rich man all dancing up a storm. The story would always spark some boyhood memory, and one story faded surely into another, so that I hardly knew when one tale ended and another began. In later years I found other versions of the tale, but I have always liked Mr. Molleré's story best.

Leo was a poor boy who lived with his *papa* in a little run-down shotgun shack. His *papa* tried hard to make a living, but after many years he was getting too old and tired to keep on working so hard. Leo saw his *papa* was just about worn out with work and worry, so one day the boy went to him and says, "I'm almost a man now. It's time for me to find work and help earn a livin'. If you can hold on a while longer, I'll go and see what I can make of myself. If my fortune is good, I'll be able to take care of you, Papa. You can spend your days fishin' or sittin' in the warm sun out on the *galerie*. You've taken care of me, now I want to do for you." Papa gave his blessing and wished his son *bonne chance.*

Leo started out and traveled all over the countryside looking for work. Times were hard and nobody wanted to hire a boy to do a man's work. One day Leo was tired and discouraged. He was just about to give up when he remembered his ol' *papa's* face. "When Papa was tired, he didn't give up," the boy thinks to himself, "and here I am actin' like a whupped pup. If I'm gonna be a man, I guess I better pick myself up and start actin' like one!" Leo started walking again. This time he wouldn't take no for an answer.

The boy came to a farm and asked the farmer if he needed a hand. Ol' farmer scratches his head and looks the boy up and down. Before he could say no, Leo claps his hands together and says, "Tell ya what I'm gonna do. Me, I'm gonna work for you for a whole year. If you don't like my work, you don't have to pay me. But if you think I've earned my pay, you can pay me then. What've ya got to lose?"

The farmer had to admit it was a good deal. The man and the boy shook hands and Leo went to work.

He proved to be the best hand the farmer ever hired. When a year had passed, Leo came to collect his wages. "If you're satisfied with my work, then I guess it's time for you to pay me and I'll be on my way."

Farmer was more than satisfied. In fact, he didn't want the boy to go. He told Leo that if he'd stay and work another year, then he'd pay the boy for two years of work when the time was up. Leo figured it was a good deal. He had no better offer and he got along just fine with the farmer.

As time went by, Leo became an even better worker, for he was growing taller and stronger and learning all the ropes. When the year was out, the boy went to collect his pay, but since the farmer still needed a hand, he asked the boy to stay on yet another year. He promised to pay him for three years when his time was up. Leo still figured it was a good deal. He trusted the old farmer, and besides, he didn't have any other offers. Times were lean and hard.

The boy worked another year. He grew even taller and stronger, and the old farmer taught him well how to bargain and trade. The year passed and he came to collect his pay. Farmer says, "You've been a good worker. I never thought a boy could do the job of a man, but I sure am glad you talked me into hirin' you. Now it's time for me to pay you and let you go on your way."

But the farmer didn't pay Leo in ordinary money. Instead, he gave him gifts that a clever boy could use to make a fortune. The first present was a gun, a special gun: no matter how it was aimed, this gun never missed its mark. The second gift was a fiddle: it played music so sweet that anybody who heard it was bound to dance until the song stopped. The last gift was a hat: Leo put it on and found that it made him invisible!

The boy told the farmer goodbye, took his gifts, and started down the road. He walked a long way, but the gifts didn't bring him any luck at all. "Well," he thinks, "if Lady Luck won't come to me, I'll just have to go and find her!"

Leo put the hat on and made himself invisible. Coming around a bend in the road, he saw a rich-lookin' man firing a gun at a strange red bird flapping across the sky.

Each shot was wide of the mark. Leo walked unseen right up to the man and heard him talking to himself. "Aw! Missed again! I've got to have that bird. It's worth a fortune! I'd pay a lot of money to get that bird down."

When Leo heard that, he knew he had caught up with Lady Luck. He took his magic hat off, and there he was standing by the rich man. He says, "I can get that bird down for you, but it'll cost you a thousand dollars." The rich man nearly jumped out of his shoes to see the boy suddenly appear at his elbow. "All right then," he agrees, "you get that bird down, and I'll pay what you ask."

Leo took aim, fired the gun, and the bird fell into a thicket of blackberry bushes. "There it is," says Leo. "Now pay me."

The rich man was greedy. He decided he would get the bird and not pay the boy a red cent. "It was a lucky shot. I coulda got it myself. You don't deserve a thousand dollars for a lucky shot!"

"All right then," says Leo, "go get the bird yourself." The man picked his way through the thorns and found the bird. But before he could get out of the thicket again, Leo started playing his magic fiddle. The song was so sweet and lively that the rich man couldn't keep his toes from tapping. Next thing he knows, his feet are dancing with a life of their own and the thorns are stickin', stickin', stickin' him! Rich man is cryin' and hollerin', "Stop, stop! I'll pay!"

Leo quit playing and the rich man stopped dancing. He paid the boy the thousand dollars, but he was mad as a wet cat. He went straight to the sheriff and had Leo arrested as a thief and a rascal. They took the boy to the judge to have a trial.

"You good-for-nothin' crook," the judge growls. "Thought you could cheat an honest man out of a thousand dollars, eh? Well, I order you to return that thousand and pay a fine of a thousand dollars more for cheatin', lyin', and bein' too smart for your britches. If you haven't got any money, then we'll throw you in the jail—or we'll take that shoot-'em-up gun, that tricky fiddle, and that magic hat for payment!"

But before they could lay hands on him or his gifts, Leo started playing the fiddle. In a second they were dancing all over the courtroom, hollering, "Stop! Stop that music!"

"I won't stop 'til ya'll pay me. A thousand for the bird, a thousand for false arrest, and a thousand for tryin' to ruin my good name."

The three men held out as long as they could until their feet were blistered and sore. "All right, we'll pay!"

Leo was too smart to let them go before they paid. He made them sign an IOU before he'd let them stop dancing. "Now, I'll expect this money to be waitin' on me when I get home. If it's not, I'm gonna put on my hat and sneak up on you, and I'll play my fiddle so fast, you'll dance 'til you melt into butter!" Then Leo packed away his fiddle and put on his hat. Quick as a wink he disappeared.

When Leo got home, his *papa* was overjoyed to see him. Three thousand dollars was waiting on him. He showed his *papa* the magic gifts. "You'll never have to work again, Papa," he says. "I've made my fortune. Your boy is gonna take care of you!"

"Ah, my son," the ol' man says, "these are fine gifts and your fortune is a blessing. But there is another gift you've earned that's more valuable than all this. You left here green and untried, but you took on the work of a man. You met all your troubles head-on and earned respect. My son, you left here as a boy, but today you come back as a man!"

Leo worked hard and had a good life. He never had to use the magic gifts again. He kept them locked away in a trunk for many years until, in time, his own son earned the gun, the fiddle, and the hat through hard work and courage.

Funny Folk Tales

Po' Boy and the Ten Thousand Dollar Egg

The folktale especially reflects the Cajun love for jokes. I wrote this story with my father-in-law, Mr. Walt Reinhart, in mind. As a young runaway during the Great Depression, he hoboed his way through Louisiana, ridin' the rails. His tales of working for food, and sometimes being cheated, helped me to grasp the spirit of the story. I originally heard the basic tale from Mr. Laurence Molleré.

There was once a young man who fell on hard times. He tried and tried to find steady work, but he just didn't have a bit of luck. After a while his clothes were ragged and he was skinny as a rake from going hungry. He was forced to sell his horse and to ride the rails looking for work. Folks got used to seeing the boy hoboing between DeQuincy and DeRidder. He was a clever fella and honest, willing to work hard for a little gumbo or some beans. But he was such a ragged and skinny-lookin' thing that people got to calling him Po' Boy, and the name stuck.

Po' Boy roamed and rambled across the countryside. One day a railroad bull put him off the train in the middle of nowhere. For three days he walked the tracks, with nothing to eat and only ditch water to drink. By the time he reached a little town, he was pretty near dead with hunger. Po' Boy came to a saloon and hit up the barkeep for a bite to eat.

"I haven't got any money, not a *sou,*" the boy says, "but me, I'm about to starve. I'd be glad to work for somethin' to eat—beans, rice, anything!"

The barkeep looks Po' Boy up and down. "Now what kinda work would I have for the likes of a bum like you? Think I'm gonna turn the bar over to a ragged boy? *Mais jamais!* I'm no fool," he growls. "I don't want the likes of you hangin' around here beggin'. I'll give ya somethin' to eat just to get rid of ya." The barkeep brought the boy a chunk of bread and a boiled egg.

"Me, I'm no bum," Po' Boy says. "I promise someday I'll come back and pay for this food." He wolfed down the food and left the saloon.

For some years after that, the boy kept riding the rails and waiting for luck to catch up with him. At last, luck found him; he got a job working for the railroad. He was so clever and such a hard worker that in time he wound up ownin' the whole outfit!

Twenty years passed. One day he remembered his promise to pay the barkeep. "I'll go back and pay him for that measly meal. He'll be surprised to see me after all this time."

Po' Boy returned to the saloon. The barkeep didn't recognize this rich man who stood before him. "What can I getcha, M'su?" he asks.

"I've come back to make good on my promise to pay you," says Po' Boy. "Twenty years ago you fed a poor hobo some bread and a boiled egg. That starvin' boy was me. I told you I was no bum and that I'd be back to pay for the food. Well, M'su, here I am. How much do I owe you for a boiled egg and a chunk of bread?"

"Hmmm," says the barkeep, "I keep a log of all money goin' in, all goin' out. Your debt's gotta be in that book." The barkeep gets the book and sure enough finds the debt from twenty years before. "Now, let's just see here a minute," he says, eyeing the rich man's gold watch and chain.

"Looks like his luck's been good," he thinks to himself. "He's a rich man now, but me, I'm still just a poor barkeep, barely gettin' by. I'm sure a rich man like him must be real grateful for me feedin' him back when he was a bum!"

"I'll just do a little figurin' here," says the barkeep out loud. He jots and jits, scratching his head and adding numbers until at last he's done. Folding his hands across his chest and grinning like a Chessie cat, he says, "Well, M'su, with interest added in for twenty years, I figure you owe me ... ten thousand dollars."

"What?" Po' Boy yells. "Ten thousand dollars for a boiled egg and a hunk of bread? Are you crazy? Just how did you come by that figure?"

"Hmmmm," says the barkeep, "the way I see it, you owe me ten thousand dollars 'cause of what mighta been. You see, M'su, if I hadn'ta fed you that boiled egg it mighta hatched. I mighta had me a fine hen who mighta laid more eggs which mighta hatched into more hens layin' more eggs, and on and on 'til I mighta made a pile of money off that one little ol' egg. So, as you can see, ten thousand dollars is very fair, *c'est vrai?"*

"Fair? Ten thousand dollars for an egg?" hollers Po' Boy. "It's robbery, and I won't pay you a cent!"

"Ah, then we can take it to court!" the barkeep hollers back. "But I better warn you, the judge is my cousin. You just meet me at the courthouse and we'll see what's what."

The two men went down to the courthouse to have a trial. First, the barkeep told his story to the judge. "Now isn't it true, Your Honor," he says with a big wink, "I mighta made a fortune off that egg if it had hatched? That one ol' egg coulda turned into hundreds of hens all layin' eggs. I mighta made a *beaucoup* of money!"

"Why, of course you mighta. Why, it's plain to see, you mighta been rich. But you gave up your chance when out of pure goodness you fed that egg to a hungry hobo," says the judge. "Now the hobo is a rich man. It's only right he should pay you back—with interest!"

Po' Boy could see he was going to have to do more to win his case than just tell the simple truth. He was a clever man and he soon had a plan. "Judge," he says, "if you'll give me 'til suppertime, I'll bring you some evidence. If my evidence doesn't change your mind, then I'll pay the ten thousand dollars."

What evidence could he bring in? No harm in waitin' a few hours, especially if the rich man was gonna pay ten thousand dollars. The judge granted Po' Boy's request.

They all left and came back at suppertime. The rich man carried a big pot of something into the courtroom. It smelled good. Why, it smelled like beans!

"Here's my evidence," says Po' Boy. "This pot of boiled beans will prove I don't owe the barkeep ten thousand dollars."

"All right then, present your evidence," says the judge.

Po' Boy set the cooked pot of beans in front of the judge. "Now, a judge has got to tell the truth, isn't that so?" he asks.

"Well, of course it is! What nonsense, what a question!"

"All right then," says Po' Boy. "Judge, just look at these boiled beans. Now I gotta question for Your Honor. If I plant these beans, will they sprout? Will they grow more beans?"

"Of course not!" the Judge sputters. "Cooked beans can't sprout and grow more beans. Whoever heard of such a thing?"

"That's right," says Po' Boy, looking at the barkeep. "Whoever did hear such a thing?" Then he reached into his pockets and brought out a good half-dozen freshly boiled eggs. "Now," he says, "take a look at these boiled eggs. Can even one of these boiled eggs hatch into a chick?"

The judge realized he and the barkeep had been tricked. "Of course a boiled egg can't hatch a chick! Whoever heard of that?" he admits, elbowing the barkeep in the ribs. The ol' judge roared with laughter, and after a while even the barkeep had to laugh at the good joke Po'

Boy played on them. The three men laughed and slapped each other on the back and the case was closed.

Pretty soon, the pot of good-smellin' beans was making all their mouths water. So they took the eggs and the beans over to the barkeep's saloon, and you can bet they passed a good time all evenin' long.

Why La Graisse (Grease) Lives in the Kitchen

This is another tale from my neighbor, Mrs. Irene Guil-
lery. Sometimes when the weather was hot-hot, she'd shoo
us kids off her porch saying, "You're not grease—you're
*not gonna melt!" I have interpreted the story as a **pour-***
***quoi** tale. One day while cleaning around my stove I*
thought, no matter how much I clean, La Graisse always
returns to get revenge!

B ack in the old country, there once lived four sisters
who were known far and wide for their beauty. They
were called La Graisse, Depomme, Pacane, and Banane.
Each sister's name matched her own special beauty:
Banane was yellow and creamy, Depomme blushed ruddy
red, Pacane was nut brown. But the little sister, La Graisse,
was the most beautiful sister of all. Her beauty shimmered
like crystal. She was dazzling.

Each day La Graisse went for a ride in her golden
carriage. She rode in the shade of a silk canopy. She never

went into the hot-hot sun for fear she might melt. One day the king's son saw La Graisse pass by in her carriage. La Graisse was so bright and shiny that the prince had to squint so he wouldn't be dazed by the light of her. It was love at first sight, and the prince made up his mind on the spot to marry La Graisse. He asked everyone he saw about her and found directions to her house. When he knocked on her door her *maman* answered.

"Madame," he says, bowing deeply, "I am in love with one of your daughters. I wish to marry her but I don't know her name. She is brighter than the sky and smoother than silk. I am the prince of this land and she will live in royal splendor if she marries me. Please, I must see her right away and ask for her hand in marriage!"

Now, La Graisse was the prettiest, but she was also the youngest. Maman didn't think it right to marry off her youngest daughter ahead of her older sisters. "La Graisse has plenty of time—she'll keep," thinks Maman, "but her sisters are older. They might spoil if they wait too much longer." Maman decides she will first show the prince her other daughters; perhaps one of them will turn his head the other way.

"Your Highness," she says, "all my daughters shine with beauty. I'm not sure which one you want to marry. I will call all of them and you can choose for yourself."

First she calls the blushing Depomme:

> *Depomme, oh! Orimomo!*
> *Depomme, oh! Orimomo!*

Depomme comes to her mother. Maman beams with pride. "Your Highness, isn't she a beauty? Just look at how red and plump she is! She'd make a fine wife, a wonderful wife."

But the prince looks her over and sees she is not the daughter he wants to marry. He shakes his head and says, "No, she is not for me. She will surely spoil much too quickly."

So Maman calls Banane, her second daughter:

> *Banane, oh! Orimomo!*
> *Banane, oh! Orimomo!*

Banane comes into the room. "Ah, Your Highness, here is a lovely bride for you," says Maman. "Just look at her lovely yellow skin! She'll make a good wife, an excellent wife."

The prince looks her over and shakes his head. "No," he says, "she'll not do at all. She'll rot all too soon."

Maman was betting on her third daughter, Pacane, to steal the prince's royal heart. She calls her:

> *Pacane, oh! Orimomo!*
> *Pacane, oh! Orimomo!*

Pacane hurries into the room. Maman smiles with pride. "Isn't she a lovely golden brown?" she says. "Why, she'd make a true wife, a loyal wife!"

The prince looks her over and shakes his head. "She will not do at all. She will shrivel and sour all too soon."

Maman was not pleased at all at the way things were going. Still, if the youngest daughter had to marry before her older sisters, she might as well marry a prince. Maybe she could help find rich husbands for her older sisters as well.

"Your Majesty, I have only one more daughter. She is very beautiful, but I must tell you she is delicate."

Maman calls her youngest daughter:

> *La Graisse, oh! Orimomo!*
> *La Graisse, oh! Orimomo!*

La Graisse comes into the room. She is radiant. The prince can't take his eyes off her.

"Ah, yes, Your Highness," says Maman, "she'll make a royal wife, a wife fit for a king!"

La Graisse and the prince were soon married. Their wedding was the event of the century. La Graisse shone in white, the most beautiful bride in the country. The prince took her to live in his palace. Everyone thought they would live happily ever after, but even true love is no sure protection from misfortune.

Each day before the prince left to go hunting he kissed La Graisse good-bye, and reminded her to stay out of the sun, for she might melt. After a while the prince's servants became jealous of her and refused to obey her wishes. La Graisse was afraid to tell her husband that she could not command her own palace. When the servants found this out, they began to force her to do their work and to wait on them. They soon discovered that La Graisse had a secret: she was afraid of fire.

One day Cook, who was a mean, jealous ol' thing, told La Graisse she would have to take over. "I'm too tired," says Cook, "so you will have to fix His Highness's supper. I know you are too scared to run whinin' to him.

If he thinks you can't run the palace, he'll be rid of you! As for me, a good cook can always get work. I might lose a job," she says with a snarl, "but you would lose a palace and your prince. Now, get cookin'! The prince will want supper when he gets back."

La Graisse begged and pleaded, but her cries fell on deaf ears. Cook only laughed harder. La Graisse stood by the huge fireplace, which was burning hot-hot. The pots boiled and bubbled. The pans popped and sizzled. Poor La Graisse began to soften and melt in all the heat. She tried to run away, but Cook made the other servants force her to stay by the fire. La Graisse begged and begged, but it was too late: she was melting, melting everywhere! Soon she covered the kitchen in a thin, shiny layer of grease.

Hearing her cries, her little pet bird flew to La Graisse and saw her predicament. He dipped his wing into her grease and flew off to find the prince. He chirped loudly until he got the prince's attention. With a flap of his wing, the little bird dropped a spatter of grease on the prince.

The prince knew La Graisse must be in terrible trouble, and he rushed back to the palace. But he arrived too late. La Graisse had already melted all over the place, nothing but a thin layer of grease on everything! The prince tried to scoop her up and pat her back together, but it was no use. No matter how he tried to scoop her up, a little of her was left sticking someplace.

Ever since then La Graisse has lived in the kitchen. Cooks can clean and clean, but she always comes back to annoy them. She sticks to everything she touches and leaves her greasy sheen wherever she goes. Her curse holds true to this day: La Graisse haunts kitchens and takes her revenge on all cooks in memory of that one wicked cook who melted her down a long, long time ago.

An Honest Man

I came across this story while doing archival research during my stay as a visiting artist for the state of North Carolina. The story has become one of my favorites for its wry humor and simple yet insightful assessment of human nature. Whenever I listen to public figures boasting of their honesty and truthfulness, I'm reminded of this story.

There was once a man who prided himself on his honesty. He never told a little bitty white lie, not even when the truth was bound to hurt somebody's feelings. To him, truth should never, ever be stretched or bent, even in fun. He thought he was the most honest man of all, and he looked down his nose at everybody else.

The old man had a beautiful daughter, *une très jolie fille.* Many young men came to court her, but her *papa* sent them all away. None of them was honest enough to suit him. The old man was determined that his daughter would marry an honest man—in short, a boy just like himself. One day a young man came calling on the old man's daughter. Papa decided to test the boy to find out if he was honest.

"Tell me," he says, *"comment ça va?* How's it going with you?"

The young man shook his head and starts to complaining. *"Ça va mal!* Not too good," he says. "My mule is a lazy good-fer-nothin', my boss is a mean ol' man who pesters me, my pockets are empty, and on top of that, I'm down in the back. I tell you the truth, times are hard!"

"Good, good, no truth-stretchin' goin' on here," thinks the old man. "Maybe I've found a man as honest as me!"

He tried another test. "Here's a story to cheer you up. I was out fishin' on the bayou one day when this great giant *goujon* big as a cow goes swimmin' by ..."

"Stop! Don't say another word!" the young man interrupted. "A giant catfish big as a cow? You're not tellin' me the truth. I don't approve of such silly stories, even if they're funny."

Papa rubs his hands together. "Wonderful! He doesn't like even a friendly joke," he thinks.

"Now for the final test. Tell me," he says, "don't you think my daughter is the most beautiful girl in the world?"

"She is pretty, all right," says the young man. "But it's not true that she's the most beautiful girl in the world. After all, she is a bit plump and her nose is a little long."

The old man was satisfied. No little white lie-tellin' was goin' on here! At last he had found a man as honest as himself. So he didn't send this young man away, but encouraged him to marry his daughter. And sure enough, some time later the couple were married, and the old man became the proud *beau-père* of an honest man.

One day, Beau-Père decided to show his son-in-law where he worked. "My boy, I know you're an honest man," he says. "I can trust you. Come with me today to work. My job is very important. It is work that requires an honest man. Maybe my boss will hire you, since you're as honest as me."

Beau-Père took his son-in-law to a great, grand building. The old man worked all alone in the place. It was his job to keep track of everybody who died in the world. He knew who would die soon and who would live for a long time. It was all told by the countless burning candles that filled the building. Each candle stood for a life. If the candle was long, it would burn for a long time and that person would have a long life. But if a person's candle was short, it would soon burn out and that poor soul would die.

There were tall candles and middle-sized candles, short candles, and candle stubs; some burned brightly, others barely flickered. The young man found his candle. It was very tall. "Where is your candle, Beau-Père?" he asks.

"Let me see," the old man says, "last time I looked it was over there. It was plenty tall too!"

"Here it is," says the son-in-law, "but look how short it is!"

"What! My candle! It's burned down almost to nothin'," the old man cries. "Oh, I haven't got long to live. I'm gonna die any day now. It's not fair! I was honest, a man of truth. Just look! Here are the candles of truth-stretchers and flatterers and storytellers. Their candles are tall and burnin' like torches. Why should they live and I die?"

The old man looked at all the tall candles and suddenly he had an idea. "Why, I don't have to die so soon. I'll just borrow a little life. We'll just cut a little bit off all those tall candles—a snip here, a snip there, just the ends. Those people will never miss them. What will they lose? A minute here, an hour there. We'll stick the pieces to my candle so that I can have a longer life!"

"Oh, *non!*" says the son-in-law. "That wouldn't be honest! Even if you cut just a snip from those tall candles it would be wrong. It doesn't matter that those people would never miss a minute, an hour. It's the principle of the thing. It's just not honest!"

"Listen, you! I'm the one who's fixin' to die, not you!" hollers Beau-Père. "It's just a drop here, a drop there. One less white lie! One less wild story! What harm can it possibly do? Probably none of these are honest people like you and me, anyway."

"Oh, *mais non,*" says the son-in-law to his *beau-père.* "I can't let you do it, because I'm an honest man. If you snip off even one little bitty piece of somebody else's candle and stick it on to yours, I'll tell! I'll go straight to your boss, and then he'll find out you're not an honest man at all. He's sure to give me your job. I'm really more suited to it. It's plain to see, I'm more honest than you!"

The old man saw there was nothing to be done. After that he stopped looking down on other people, for now he knew he wasn't better than anybody else, and honesty wasn't always the best policy. The old man had discovered truth. From then on until his candle burned out, he was a changed man. He often smiled when he was really sad; he told funny, tall stories to cheer a worried

soul; and he found it easy to see beauty in the plainest face.
He didn't live long, but he lived better.

Jean Sot and Bull's Milk

There are many tales about Jean Sot, or Foolish John. Unlike Jack, the hero of the Appalachian mountain tales, Jean Sot isn't clever at all, but is as slow-witted and gullible as they come. He is always getting into trouble in the silliest ways. His poor **maman** *doesn't know what to do with him. But Jean Sot isn't always a loser; sometimes he wins by pure luck. Mr. Laurence Molleré liked to tell this story in between spitting out long streams of tobacco juice into a Coca-Cola bottle. He'd get a sly grin on his face and hold out the slimy bottle and say, "Wanna Coke?" I never took him up on his offer—after all, I wasn't as silly-headed as Jean Sot!*

Down around Mamou, there was once a boy who was so foolish that everybody called him Jean Sot, Foolish John. He and his *maman* were dirt poor, and he was less than no help at all. It seemed like Jean Sot just couldn't do anything right. Everything he touched ended in ruin, and he believed any silly story he was told. His *maman* would shake her head and sigh, "Oh, that boy must have moss between his ears!"

The people in his village loved to tease and play jokes on him. They'd say, "Jean Sot, the sky is fallin'!" The poor thing would run and hide, sure the world was ending for true. But their best joke was to ask, "Hey, boy, whatcha gonna be when you all grown up?" Jean Sot loved that question. He would grin from ear to ear and say, "Me, I'm gonna marry the prettiest girl and be the richest man in all the parish." How the people laughed and laughed!

In time, the foolish boy became a foolish young man. One day as he was walking down the road, he passed by a big, fancy house. A beautiful girl was sitting up on the *galerie,* combing out her golden hair. She had the face of an angel but the brains of a duck. She was every inch as foolish as Jean Sot! Wouldn't you know, those two took one look at each other and fell right in love.

Jean Sot begged her to marry him. The girl says, "Oh, yes, *cher, mais oui!* But you must ask Papa for my hand!" The foolish boy ran to the girl's daddy, little knowing that this was the richest man in the parish, and asked to marry his daughter. But the rich man knew all too well about Jean Sot, and he had not the least intention of seeing his only child marry a fool, much less a poor one. Still, he thought it might be a good joke to play along and see just how foolish Jean Sot could be.

"Hmm," says the rich man, pretending to think it over, "I don't know if you are good enough for my daughter. Maybe you can prove yourself to me?"

"Oh, *oui,* Papa, anything you say!"

"Well, then, take this silver flask and fill it up for me."

"What do you want?" asks Jean Sot. "Wine, whis-key?"

"Non," says the rich man, keeping a straight face. "Take this flask and fill it up with ... bull's milk. That's right! If you can fill this flask with the milk of a bull, then you can marry my daughter, and all my wealth will be yours someday."

So Jean Sot eagerly took the flask, and away he went down the road to find a bull to milk. He ran until he came to the countryside. There in a pasture, sure enough, was a big ol' mean-lookin' bull.

He walked right up to that bull and looked him over, trying to figure where to get started. But ol' bull was getting madder and madder, pawing the ground, shaking his horns. The next thing you know, he was charging and Jean Sot was running for his life. He just barely escaped!

That evening Jean Sot thought harder than he'd ever thought in his life. Suddenly, it came to him. The girl's father had tricked him! Now, after a lifetime of being the target of everyone's practical jokes, even Jean Sot had learned a little something, you see. He thinks, "The time has come to show them all." Soon he had made a plan.

Late that night, with a little hatchet in hand, he went back to the rich man's house and shimmied up a slippery willow tree growing beside the man's bedroom window. He perched on a limb and took to chopping on that tree, chip-chop, chip-chop, chip-chop. All the while he's moanin' and groanin', "Oh, *mon pauvre papa!* Oh, my poor *papa!"*

Before long, the whole neighborhood comes running to see what all the commotion's about.

The shutters of the rich man's window fly open and he hollers out, "Jean Sot, is that you? What the devil are you doin', choppin' on my tree and moanin' to raise the dead in the middle of the night? I know you're foolish, but I didn't know you was crazy too!"

"Oh, my poor *papa*, he's havin' such a hard time of it," says Jean Sot. "This bark'll make a good tea, don't ya know, and help 'im get stronger."

"What's the matter with your *papa*, boy?" asks the rich man, taken aback. "Is he sick-sick? Has he got the fever?"

"Oh no, it's much worse than that!" says Jean Sot. "Never has a poor man had it so rough. You see, tonight my *papa* gave birth—to twins!"

"Mon Dieu!" the rich man exclaims. "Did he have boys, or girls, or one of each?"

With that, Jean Sot started in to laughin' so hard he nearly fell out of the tree. The neighbors were slappin' each other on the back and sputterin'. Well, the rich man realized he'd been had, and he starts to cussin'.

"Of all the … Jean Sot, you better get outta that tree and quit tellin' lies 'fore I get my shotgun after you!"

"I don't think I'd be talkin' 'bout lyin' if I was you," says Jean. "I don't want to call you a liar, but if you say a bull can give milk, then my *papa* can give birth to twins, for true!"

The rich man was ashamed. His neighbors had witnessed the whole thing, and so he was forced to hold up his end of the bargain or be ridiculed as a greater fool than Jean Sot.

And so, just as he had predicted, Jean married the prettiest girl and became the richest man in the whole parish. The people started thinking that he must really be smart-smart after all. They even made him captain of the the Mardi Gras riders. It just goes to show that even the greatest of fools can sometimes become a leader.

Jean Sot and the Giant Cows

*I heard this tale from Shirley Bergeron, a well-known Cajun musician and songwriter. We met at a Cajun music festival in Rhode Island where we were both performing. We struck up a conversation, and I soon realized Mr. Bergeron was not only a great musician but a natural-born **raconteur** as well.*

Everybody around Mamou was surprised when that foolish boy Jean Sot married the prettiest girl in town and got rich to boot. They had always figured he'd never amount to a hill of beans. His good fortune made them all think he was smarter than he seemed. But the fact of the matter was, Jean Sot was just as foolish as ever. His pretty wife wasn't too smart-smart herself, and their two heads together were twice as foolish as Jean Sot's one moss-filled head by itself!

One day Jean Sot came running to his wife, out of breath with excitement. *"Chère,"* he says, "guess what? We got some new neighbors comin'!"

"How do you know that?" she asks.

"I just saw one of those newfangled pick-em-up trucks pull up next to our land! Looks like they got some big ol' fence posts, too. Must be they're gonna put up a fence and pen up some cows. Maybe they'll be milk cows. Just think o' all that milk and butter our neighbors'll give us! Well, I better get on back over there and keep an eye on things. After all, I am the richest man in the parish. They might need my advice."

Jean Sot runs through his field over to where the pick-em-up truck is parked. He stands there gawking at the machine and watching the men unload the poles. Now, Jean Sot had never been beyond the next parish. He'd never even seen a truck up close. Folks around there were simple country people who still plowed with mules and traveled by wagon. Jean Sot had heard about such things as electricity and the telephone, but he had never seen such amazing things with his own eyes.

He figured folks were just teasing him, trying to pull his leg as usual. But now that he was rich, he didn't fall for their old jokes anymore. They expected him to believe that a little glass ball would just light up the darkness? No oil or wick? Aaiiee! That was a good one! Or some silly sounding box they called a telephone thatcha talked into and folks could hear ya talkin' to 'em from miles away? Ha! He'd have to have a head full o' mud to swallow that one!

So, when the men started pulling long-long poles out of that big pick-em-up truck, his eyes grew big as supper plates. He watched as the workmen dug deep holes and put the pole ends into them. Then with ropes and pulleys they raised the poles up until they stood tall and straight as a good-sized tree.

Jean Sot plucked up his courage and walks over to the workmen. *"Comment ça va?* Hey, boys, what ya'll gonna do with those big ol' poles?" he asks, all nervous-like.

The workmen, who were strangers to those parts, looked at Jean Sot with raised eyebrows. "Why, we gonna string some wire, of course," says the big boss man. Sure enough, just then the workmen unloaded some big spools of thick wire. Jean Sot took one look and started to shaking in his boots. He watched as the men climbed up the poles and commenced stringing wire between those huge fence posts.

This was too much! Jean Sot runs off yellin' at the top of his lungs: "Aaiiee! Oh, *chère!* Start packin'! We got to get outta here, *vite-vite!"*

Jean Sot runs home like a crazy man. He tears into his house goin' ninety miles a minute, and just about scares the tar out of his poor wife.

"Jean!" she yells. "What's the matter for you? Why are you yellin' we gotta get packed and go? Me, I'm not goin' nowhere. Wild horses couldn't drive me from *ma maison."*

"Ah, *chère!* It's not horses we gotta worry about, it's cows! Giant cows! We gotta get outta here fast. They're liable to break loose and stampede us. I don't wanna be killed by no giant cow!"

His wife stares at Jean Sot like he's got crawfish crawlin' out of his ears. "What in the world are you talkin' about? Giant cows? Why, somebody must be tryin' to play a joke on you."

"Oh, no," he says, "I saw it all with my own two eyes. They're puttin' up a huge fence out there. You should see those fence posts, tall as a tree, I tell ya. And that fence wire they're stringin', thick as my wrist. They're fencin' in giant cows! I'm not livin' next to no giant cows, *mais non!* Why, we'd never get a minute of peace for worryin' about those monsters breakin' through that fence and tramplin' us into *couche-couche.*"

"Well, I can't believe any such thing as giant cows," says his wife. "I'm gonna go see for myself before I pack up and leave."

"Oh, no!" exclaims Jean Sot. "I can't let you go by yourself, it's too dangerous! Those giant cows can't be far. They're probably herdin' them this way right now. If you don't believe me, then I'll take you over there and show you for true. You'll hush your mouth then and get to packin', I bet!"

Jean Sot and his wife trotted through their field, arguing all the way. When they came up some distance from the pick-em-up truck they stopped, and Jean Sot pointed. "There," he says, "look for yourself. Do you not see those tall-tall poles? Do you not see that thick-thick wire runnin' between 'em? I tell you one thing, *chère,* they are not buildin' that fence for any ordinary cow. Whatever kind of animal they're gonna pen up in that fence has got to be some kind of a giant!"

"Oh, *cher!*" his wife cries. "You are right. It is a fence for giant cows. Quick-quick! Back to the house to get packed up. We're not gonna live next door to no giant cows!"

Jean Sot and his wife ran back home, hollerin' like there was a giant cow already chasing them.

The workmen out by the pick-em-up truck watched the man and woman yellin' and runnin' away like chickens with their heads chopped off. "What do ya suppose they're so afraid of?" asks one fella.

"Sure beats me," says the big boss man. "Looks like they'd be glad we're puttin' up these poles and stringin' this wire. After all, now they gonna have electricity, not to mention the telephone. Oh well, you know how some people are just scared silly of anything new."

The workmen shook their heads and went back to work, putting up the poles and wire, bringing electricity and the telephone to the country folks at last.

St. Antoine the Wonder Worker

*I heard this tale at a **gumbo ya-ya** hen party. It was a rainy day and I was wishing out loud that it wouldn't rain anymore. An old lady who was visiting Miss Irene says to me, "Ah, **chère,** you better be careful what you wish for..." Then she told this story that she had heard from her **maman.** I also heard a version of the tale from an old man who sold candles and powders in a little **gris-gris** shop. We talked awhile about how prayers come true, although not always in quite the way we expect. "Yeah," he says, "when ya pray, ya got to be real sepific!"*

Bella was a poor orphan girl who lived with her *grandmaman.* She was a pretty girl with large, dark eyes and rosy lips, but nobody ever noticed Bella because she was very shy and quiet. The other children were cruel to the girl. They made fun of her worn, ill-fitting, hand-me-down clothes, and nicknamed her Scarecrow. The children's cruel words hurt Bella and made her feel ashamed. But as she grew into a young woman, her wise old *grandmaman* taught her to value a strong spirit and a good heart over all the pretty things that money could buy.

Bella reached a marrying age, but no young men came to call. Their eyes were blinded by her coarse clothing. They could not see that beneath those rags beat a heart of gold.

In the evenings Bella sat out on the *galerie,* sewing and listening to *grandmaman's* stories. In the old woman's tales anything could happen: wishes came true and the saints heard every prayer. Bella listened and wished that her prayers would be granted. She prayed that the young man she secretly loved would one day love her, too.

Bella had lost her heart to Marcel, the son of the richest man in the parish. But it was not the young man's wealth that she loved; it was his quiet strength and kind ways. The other girls flirted and teased Marcel, trying to win a rich husband, but Marcel was smart, and he saw that they were greedy. He longed to find a woman who would love him whether he was rich or poor. Each day Marcel walked past Bella's poor shack on his way to town. He never noticed the quiet, shy girl sitting on the porch, and never saw the dark eyes that followed him with love.

Grandmaman knew that her granddaughter was in love with Marcel, but she hoped the girl would get over him. The young man was so rich it would take a miracle for him to fall in love with the poor girl called Scarecrow.

One day Bella came to her *grandmaman* and revealed her secret prayer. "Grandmaman, what can I do to win the love of Marcel? You tell me stories of the saints and their miracles; surely the saints can help me, too. You're so wise, Grandmaman. Tell me what I gotta do to have my prayers answered."

Grandmaman thought a long time. She didn't want to give the girl false hope. "You've lost your heart to the young man. Pray to St. Antoine. He is called the Wonder Worker, for he is the saint who finds what has been lost. Pray to him, *chère,* and in time your prayer will be answered."

Bella prayed day and night for the love of Marcel. Each day she followed him with her eyes, though he never noticed her. After many, many prayers she asked her grandmother for more advice. "Grandmaman, I pray and pray but nothin' happens. Marcel doesn't even know I'm alive. What more can I do?"

Grandmaman looked into the girl's eyes. She saw that Bella was truly in love with Marcel. "St. Antoine hears so many prayers," she says. "Maybe his ears are stopped up. Sometimes we gotta help the saints hear our prayers by speakin' up for ourselves and takin' action! This evening bring me the wooden statue of St. Antoine from his shelf. We're gonna pray again, but louder, much louder!"

Bella did as her grandmother requested and brought the statue to her. The old woman held an auger in her hand. Bella looked at the tool and asks, "Grandmaman, what we gonna do to St. Antoine?"

"St. Antoine's ears are stopped up with prayers," Grandmaman says. "We are gonna bore holes in his ears so he can hear your prayer!"

Just then Grandmaman saw Marcel coming down the road. In a big voice she announced, "We will now drill out the ears of St. Antoine!" She made a great show of working on the statue's ears. All the ruckus attracted

Marcel's attention, and he was full of curiosity. Why were those two women drilling holes in St. Antoine's ears? Marcel hid behind a tree, watching and listening.

When Grandmaman was sure Marcel was paying attention, she quit drilling. "Now," she says, "say your prayer, Bella, say it loud and clear."

Bella lowered her head and spoke in a sweet voice. "Oh, dear St. Antoine, hear my prayer. I've lost my heart to Marcel. I love him so much. St. Antoine, you know I love him, not his money. I would marry him if he was the poorest man on earth. Let him see past my rags to my heart—it is true and beats only for him. It is said that you can find whatever is lost. St. Antoine, my heart is lost to Marcel. Please let him find it and return it to me. If he does not, my heart will be lost forever. I'll never love another. Amen."

Marcel was so astonished to hear Bella's prayer that at last he looked beyond her poverty and saw the beauty of her dark eyes and the goodness of her heart. And he knew that his own prayers had been answered. Without hesitation, Marcel went to Bella and placed her hand in his own hand.

Grandmaman quietly left the love-struck couple alone. She put the statue of St. Antoine on his shelf. Her old eyes twinkled as she looked out the window at Bella and Marcel gazing into each other's eyes. She began to pray.

"Dear St. Antoine, thank you for listenin'. Help these two children always remember to be very careful what they pray for, 'cause in life, as in stories, prayers have a way of comin' true. Amen."

Roclore and His Bag of Tricks

My elderly friend Miss Rosella told me this story shortly before she passed away. Even though her eyes were dimmed by blindness, they seemed to twinkle whenever she told this tale. There are several variants of the story in Louisiana folklore, as well as a number of other stories about the trickster Roclore, sometimes called Roclos.

Roclore was a rascal and a trickster. No one escaped his sly jokes and sharp wit, not even the king himself! Now, it happened that Roclore fell in love with the king's beautiful daughter. She favored the young man as well and wished to marry him, but her *papa* wouldn't hear of such a thing. "That rascal marry my *p'tite fille?*" asks the king. *"Mais jamais,* never! He isn't royal or rich enough to marry a princess." The king forbade Roclore to court his daughter, but the young man was in love, and he continued to visit the princess in secret.

One day the king discovered Roclore in the palace garden, and this made him madder than a stirred up hornet. "What are you doin' comin' around here," he demands, "after I told you to stay away from my daughter? This time you've gone too far. I'm gonna get rid of you once and for all."

The king ordered his servants to catch Roclore and tie him up in a big bag. "I'm gonna take you down to the river and throw you in. I'm gonna drown you just like an ol' mangy, prowlin' cat!"

Roclore was worried, but he didn't waste any energy trying to fight his way out of the bag. Instead he sat and figured out a way to trick the king.

On the way down to the river the king decides to stop at the saloon and take a little refreshment. He goes inside and starts bragging about how he's outsmarted that ol' foxy Roclore once and for all. The king left the young man sitting in the wagon, all tied up in the big bag. Roclore gets an idea. He starts to moanin' and hollerin' as loud as he can, "Oh, I don't want to, no, I don't want to!"

Pretty soon an old shepherd comes by with his flock of sheep. He hears all the ruckus and stops to look at the bag. "Who's in there," he says, "and what is it you don't want to do?"

"It's me, poor Roclore! The king has trapped me in this bag 'cause he wants to make me marry his daughter. Oh, I don't care if she is beautiful. I don't care that I'll be rich and inherit the king's money. I just want to be free! If only somebody would take my place."

"Say now," says the old fella, "that sounds like a pretty good deal to me! I wouldn't mind marryin' up with a beautiful, rich princess. I'm awful tired of tendin' these ol' sheep. I'd sure like to be rich. How about you take my sheep, and I'll take your place?"

"Quick, then," says Roclore, "open up the bag and change places with me. You can marry the princess instead of me."

The greedy man opened the bag and Roclore jumped out. The old fella climbs in and the young man ties him up in the bag. "Now remember," says Roclore, "you got to pretend that you're me. Don't let on that the real Roclore has escaped."

The young man quickly led the sheep away and put them in a pen. Then he went down to the river and hid himself so he could see what would happen.

The king came out of the saloon and drove the wagon to the Mississippi. He pushed the big bag out of the wagon. Inside the sack the old fella is hollerin' just like Roclore had done, "I don't want to. Oh, I don't want to!"

"Hush up, Roclore!" ol' King yells. "It's too late now. You thought you could outsmart the king, eh? Well, let's see ya trick your way out of this bag." With that, the king swings the bag around and around and throws it into the muddy river with a great big splash! When the king was satisfied that he had drowned Roclore, he headed back for his castle.

A week or so passes, and one day here comes Roclore, right through the king's garden, driving a big flock of sheep. Ol' King is about to choke, he's so mad. "Roclore, what are you doin' back?" he yells. "I thought I got rid of you! And what are you doin' with those sheep?"

"Oh, you nearly drowned me for true," Roclore shouts back, "but you didn't throw me far enough. I just floated along till I wiggled outta the bag. Lucky for me, I landed in a gold mine. If only I could've stayed down longer, I would've come back with a whole herd of cattle besides these sheep. I tell you, just six feet under there's more riches than even you can imagine! King, I gotta thank you for throwin' me in. A few more trips and I'll be richer than you."

Now, if there was anything the king couldn't stand, it was the idea of somebody getting richer than him. He was a greedy ol' thing and hot-headed to boot. He fell for Roclore's fishy story, hook, line, and sinker! "Roclore, you say it's only six feet or so down? Couldn't you share your good luck with me? After all, you really have me to thank for your fortune."

"Well, all right then," says Roclore, "I'll show you the spot. Come climb into my bag and I'll throw you in the river."

The king comes down and climbs into the big bag. Roclore ties it up good, and off they go to the river. When they get there, Roclore picks up the bag and swings it round and round, then he lets it sail. That bag falls with a big splash, way out in the middle of the river.

"Well, that's that," says Roclore, *"c'est tout!"* Roclore married the princess and together they raised a herd of happy, clever children. And as far as anybody knows, ol' King wiggled out of that sack and is still floating around in that muddy river, looking for a Mississippi gold mine!

The Killer Mosquitoes

My grandmother told me a simple version of this tale. Later, I found several variations between Southeast Texas and Georgia. I especially like this story because it reminds me of an English friend from Liverpool who once stayed with my family in Nashville, Tennessee. One night we sat outside with the fireflies flitting around us. I noticed that he jumped whenever a firefly lit up in the air beside him. At last he asks in his cockney accent, "Do these things bite?" I couldn't resist pulling his leg a bit. "Oh, they won't bite—as long as you sit perfectly still." For the rest of the evening he sat as still as a statue!

There were once three Irishmen called O'Leary, O'Bleary, and O'Neary who decided to leave the old country and come to Louisiana. They'd heard about the rich, black, delta dirt and the great plantations. They figured they'd find some work, save their money, and start farming. They'd grow sugar cane and cotton, beans and rice, everything but potatoes—they were just sick and tired of eating potatoes. O'Leary, O'Bleary, and O'Neary took passage on a ship bound for New Orleans. After weeks at sea, the Irishmen arrived in Louisiana at last. They got off the boat and started walking around to see what they could find for themselves.

They kept to the river, looking for a plantation where they could find work. Before long they were lost in the middle of the river bottom. Everywhere there were only swamp woods as far as they could see. The *mousse* hung down from the trees like an old man's beard, and *boscoyo* rose up from the water like knobby knees. Alligators snapped at them and cottonmouth snakes hissed. But they weren't afraid, for they'd heard about the strange creatures that lived in La Louisianne: fish with cat whiskers and big as a man; giant snapping turtles; *pichou,* the bobcat that screamed like a woman. They fancied they knew all they needed to know to get by, so on they tramped, deeper and deeper into the swamp.

The sun began to sink low, so they decided they better make camp for the night. They found a little sheltered piece of dry ground and settled down there. The sun set and darkness fell. The three Irishmen were so tired they were soon fast asleep. They'd slept only a few winks when suddenly they woke up howling and slapping at their faces and arms. A high, whining sound whirred in their ears. They were being attacked by some kind of tiny beasts with a bite like the stick of a needle!

"What is it?" hollers O'Leary.

"I dunno, but it bites like the devil!" O'Bleary yells.

"I can't see it," says O'Neary, "but I can hear it whinin' for our blood!"

All night long the Irishmen slapped and cursed at the little monsters. When morning came they were red-eyed and covered with itchy red bumps. At last they got a look at the beasts that had nearly eaten them alive. They didn't know what to make of the little bloodthirsty creatures. They had never heard of mosquitoes!

"We better get out of here before they come back with their mates and kill us for good," says O'Leary. O'Bleary and O'Neary agreed, and they hurried away as quickly as they could through the swamp.

Well, the three men didn't have a notion of where they were going, and they wound up on the river right back where they started. They'd been walking in a circle. They turned in the opposite direction and walked until the sun was low in the sky. A little deserted cabin lay before them, perched on the river bank. They thought it looked like a good place to spend the night.

The three Irishmen barred the door and pulled the shutters. "We'll be safe here from those creatures. They'll not bite us tonight," they said. They settled in, with stomachs growling and the three of them just itchin' all over. They were dog-tired, and pretty soon they fell fast asleep. O'Neary's snoring woke up O'Leary, and when he sat up he saw blinking lights buzzing about the room.

"Wake up, mates!" he shouts. "Those blood-suckin' devils are back!" The others woke up trembling. "They mean to kill us for sure!" hollers O'Neary. "Faith and begorra!" shouts O'Bleary. "Look! They brought lanterns so they could see us and suck us dry. Run for it, boys! Aaiieegghh!"

The three Irishmen were running so wildly to get out of that cabin that they broke the door down. They didn't know that the blinking, buzzing lights in the cabin were only harmless *mouches à feu,* fireflies.

O'Leary, O'Bleary, and O'Neary didn't stop running until they got back to New Orleans, where they took the first ship they could find back to Ireland. After that, they never minded eating potatoes at every blessed meal. For at least at home they were safe from those whining, needle-nosed, lantern-carrying, blood-sucking, killer mosquitoes!

Pierre and the Angel of Death

My friend, Miss Rosella, told me this tale as I brushed and braided her long white hair. I will never forget how the story made her laugh, and how she said Pierre reminded her of her own late husband.

There was once a man called Pierre who lived with his wife Alida in a little *cabane* on the bank of the bayou. They didn't have much money, but they had a tight roof and good neighbors who'd help them out, and they had each other. Alida was a good-natured woman, full of laughter and plump as a feather pillow. But Pierre was skinny as a rake and nervy as a gnat. He worried about every little thing.

If it rained, Pierre predicted flood; if the sun was shining, he worried the well was going to run dry. If he got the sniffles, look out—he was certain he was about to die. Pierre was convinced that life was miserable and that any day now he was fixin' to be a goner.

"Ohhh!" he'd groan and whine. "It won't be long now, Alida. Death is gonna come and take me away, out o' this misery. Ohhh, *pauvre moi!* poor me

"Pierre," she'd say, "you're healthy as a horse. Come, *cher,* have a big bowl of my good gumbo. That'll fix you up for sure."

"What?" says Pierre. "You'd give gumbo to a dyin' man? Are you tryin' to get rid of your husband?"

Pierre complained day in, day out, until one evening Alida couldn't stand his whining any longer. "Ohhh," he starts in moanin', "if only death would spare me this misery. Surely any day now death will come and take me from this terrible life."

"Shh!" Alida hushes him. "Stop talkin' like that!" She looks about the cabin and says in a loud whisper, "*She* might be around to hear you and answer your call."

"Who do you mean?" asks Pierre.

"Why, Madame de la Mort!" says Alida with big eyes. "The Angel of Death! I don't think a man in your condition oughta be temptin' Madame de la Mort with idle talk of dyin'."

"What do you mean, my 'condition'?" he asks nervously.

"Ah, Pierre, you look awful!" Alida shakes her head with a worried look. "Your eyes are glassy," she says, "and your cheeks are pale. You tremble like a ghost."

Pierre's eyes are as big as supper plates. He puts his hand to his brow. "It's true!" he wails. "Me, I'm sick-sick."

"Quick, *cher,*" says Alida, "lie down and sleep. I will go get the *traiteur.* It is a long way, but maybe I'll bring him back in time to save you." Alida made out like she was gonna go fetch the healer. But instead, she hid herself out in the corn shed.

She waited there until she was sure Pierre was fast asleep. Then she took a length of heavy chain and crept softly back into the dark house. She climbed up into the loft and hid herself in the shadows. Down below, Pierre was fast asleep, snoring loud enough to wake the dead.

Alida starts to rattling that heavy chain, and in a thin, high voice she calls out, "Ooohhhhh! Ooohhhh!"

Pierre wakes up trembling. His teeth are chattering so hard that he can barely talk. "Who—who—who's th—th—there?" he stammers out into the darkness.

"*C'est moi*," moans Alida, "Madame de la Mort!"

"Wh—what do ya w—want?" asks Pierre.

Alida moans, "Ooohhhh! I've been called by the sighs and complaints of one who wishes to leave this world before his time. I've come to grant him his wish. Ooohhhh!"

Pierre gasps, "Who—who have you c—c—come for?"

"I come for Pierre," she wails, "Pierre who calls for death before his time."

"But wh—what if this Pierre ... wh—what if he's ch—changed his mind? What if he don't really wanta die?"

"Ooohhhh!" she moans. "Too bad. Once I snare him with my heavy, cold chain, he is mine forever. Ooohhh!"

Pierre was scared to death by this time. He was shaking like a leaf and white as a sheet.

"Who are youuuuu?" she demands. "Are you Pierre, are you the one I seeeek?"

"Oh, n—no, I'm not Pierre. Uh—uh—Pierre is not here!" he stutters.

"Ooohhhh! Where is Pierre?" she moans.

"P—P—Pierre is—is at the neighbor's house. Yes, that's it! Pierre is at the neighbor's house! Why, he's at the *fais-dodo. Mais oui.* He'll be dancin' all night, he won't be back 'til early mornin'."

"Ahhhh," she says, "then I will wait here for Pierre until dawn."

Pierre nearly choked. "Oh, *non!* Uh—uh—then me, I'll go get Pierre. Y—yes, that's wh—what I'll do, I'll go tell him the Angel of Death is here waitin' for him!"

With that, Pierre hit the floor running so fast that he broke the door down trying to get out of that cabin. Behind him he could hear Madame de la Mort laughing like a she-devil. He was so scared that he hid out in the swamp all night. He was more terrified of the Angel of Death than he was of any ol' gator or cottonmouth!

In the morning he came back red-eyed and covered with mud, tippy-toein' up the steps of the *galerie,* just in case Madame de la Mort might still be hanging around.

Suddenly, he felt a hand on his shoulder. "Aaiiee!" he hollers.

"Pierre, it's only me, your Alida," she says. "Where have you been? I was so worried that maybe you died and they took you away!"

Pierre told Alida all about the visit of Madame de la Mort. "You do believe me, don't you?" he asks, all big-eyed.

"Of course I believe you, *cher,*" she says with an innocent look.

After that, Pierre stopped complaining all the time. He fattened up on Alida's good gumbo and wasn't sick a day for the rest of his life. He quit worrying so much about the hereafter and started living the here-right-now.

Dead Men Don't Talk

This tale of two gambling tricksters and a practical joke gone haywire has always tickled me. I used epitaphs from South Louisiana graveyards to interpret the ending of the story. There, Cajun people often decorate and whitewash the vaults of their loved ones. Kind words (and some not so kind words) are often chiseled into the stone. One of my favorite inscriptions is the one on my ol' great-great uncle's tombstone. After a family dispute over who was going to pay for his fancy stone marker, the relatives who wound up footin' the bill added a new inscription for all to see: "This stone bought and paid for by Maud and Leon."

There was once a fella who loved to play practical jokes. He'd go to any length to get the last laugh. One day he decided to pull a prank on his ol' *padnat,* the shoemaker. He made a bet with his friend. *"Mon ami,"* says the joker, "I bet you are too scared to sit up all night with the dead. Why, I wager you'd be runnin' for the door long before midnight!"

The shoemaker says, "Of course I'm not scared of a corpse. I could sit up all night with a hundred dead bodies—it wouldn't bother me in the least."

"All right then," says the joker, "I dare you to sit up all night with just one corpse. There's a body down at the church, all laid out in a coffin, waitin' to be buried tomorrow. You go and sit with that corpse tonight. If you stay put 'til dawn, I'll pay you a hundred dollars—but if you run out before mornin', you owe me a hundred dollars." The other fella took the bet and agreed to go to the church that very night.

Now, the joker figured he'd made an easy bet. He was already thinking about how he was going to spend the money he was about to win off his buddy. He thinks to himself, "There is no way that shoemaker is gonna last the night, not if I have anything to do with it. Me, I know a way to run him outta that church, if it doesn't scare him to death first."

So that evening the joker put on a dead man's shroud. Then he smudged his eyes with charcoal until they looked hollow and dark. Finally, he dusted himself all over with white flour so that he looked pale and ghostly. When darkness fell, he snuck up unseen to the church. Inside it was dim and gloomy, with just a few candles flickering and casting eerie shadows on the walls. Meanwhile the wind had risen and was whistling and rattling at the door. The pine coffin he had made just yesterday lay empty, waiting for a body. "Perfect!" he says, with a satisfied look around the church.

Just then, footsteps. Quick-quick, he climbs into the coffin and pulls the lid to, leaving it open just a crack so he can keep an eye on his buddy.

The shoemaker steps cautiously into the church and peers at the coffin. "Well," he says, "I'm not gonna look inside this pine box. If ya seen one dead body, ya seen 'em all. But if I'm gonna be here all night I might as well get caught up on my work." The shoemaker pulls out some unfinished boots and some tools, sits down on top of the coffin, and begins tacking boot heels with his little hammer. Tap, tap, tap, tap, tap goes the hammer.

Inside the coffin, the joker waits and waits for his friend to get curious and open the lid. But the little hammer just goes on and on: tap, tap, tap, tap, tap, tap.

"Hmm," thinks the joker, "this isn't goin' well at all. He was supposed to open the coffin to see who died—then I'd sit up and scare the tar outta him! But all he does is tap, tap, tap with that blessed hammer. I'm just gonna have to get him to open up this coffin."

He thinks a bit and gets an idea. On the inside of the coffin he starts rapping: rap, rap, rap.

But the shoemaker just keeps right on tap, tap, tapping and doesn't hear the knocks. The joker thinks, "He must be hard of hearing. If he don't open this lid soon, I'll run out of breathing air!" He starts rapping again, louder this time: rap, rap, rap!

Now the shoemaker hears it and stops tapping. He gets up and goes to the church door, opens it, and looks around. "Nobody out here," he says. "Guess it was just the wind rattlin' the door." He sits down and pretty soon he's hard at work again with his hammer: tap, tap, tap, tap, tap. The joker raps again, this time as loud as he can: RAP, RAP, RAP, RAP, RAP!

The shoemaker's hammer stops tapping. "What was that?" he asks, looking at the coffin. He stands up, hammer in hand, and slowly raises the lid.

Suddenly, the joker bolts up and moans, "A man sittin' with the dead ought not work."

The shoemaker jumps back, startled. "Well," he says, gathering his wits, "dead men shouldn't talk." And with his little cobbler's hammer he gives the joker a big TAP— right on the head, and kills him cold.

"That'll teach a dead man not to talk!" he says. "But wait a minute. Somethin' funny is goin' on here." He takes a closer look at the man dressed up like a corpse and now a dead man for true. "Ah, I've killed *mon padnat!*" he cries out. "Oh, no! What am I gonna do?"

The shoemaker thinks for a minute. "I know," he says, "I'll bury him. After all, he's all ready to go."

So the shoemaker goes out into the dark night and digs a grave in the church cemetery. Then he drags the coffin out beside the hole. "Oh," he thinks, "I've forgotten to nail the lid down."

He fetches his hammer and some nails. "I'm sorry ol' friend," he says, "I guess your joke backfired. This is one time you won't get the last laugh."

He bends down in the darkness and starts driving nails into the coffin. When it's nailed down tight, he heaves until he pushes it over the edge and it falls into the grave. But at the last second, just before the pine box lands with a thud, the shoemaker feels something choking him. Too late he realizes what he has done.

"Oh, *non!* I've nailed my tie to the coffin!"

Next morning, the people found a strange sight. There was the shoemaker, choked to death by his own tie nailed to the coffin. Inside the pine box lay his friend, all dressed up like a corpse and dead as a doornail, with a big knot on his head. The people soon figured out the joker's prank and what had happened to the shoemaker.

They buried the two side by side. On the joker's tombstone they carved, "He Who Laughs Last, Laughs Best." And on the shoemaker's stone they wrote, "Dead Men Don't Talk."

Ghost Stories

Fifolet

*When I was a teenager there was a spot where young couples went in hopes of getting a look at the **fifolet** lights—known elsewhere as the will o' the wisp, or just plain ol' swamp gas. For the most part, the only fire out there was the sparks of young love. Occasionally, though, somebody would swear to having seen the **fifolet,** and a great many stories grew up about the eerie, floating lights. I have also been told that a sighting of a **fifolet** indicates that a treasure is buried nearby: follow the **fifolet** and it will lead you to hidden riches. Growing up with this story, however, never made me too inclined to follow a **fifolet.** The lights were scary enough from a distance.*

Down around the great Atchafalaya swamp, there was an old man called Medeo, who had mastered the evil arts. At night this wizard would go in secret to a corn shed, and once inside, he'd shimmy out of his skin like a snake, roll it up, and hide it in a shadowy corner. Then, by the power of his evil spell, the wizard would change himself into a *fifolet*, a burning, shining ball of blue and white flames. He'd float out to the swamp, dancing and bobbing through the darkness, tempting all to follow him to destruction and death.

People in the village began to disappear. Others followed the *fifolet* and fell under the wizard's spell. They became like the living dead, forced to slave for Medeo and obey his every command.

In the village there was a young woman called Zula. She was curious as a cat. What was happenin' to the people? They had once laughed and danced, but now they only stared like owls and walked with shuffling feet. Zula kept her eyes and ears open. Soon she saw that old Medeo entered the corn shed as a man ... but left as a *fifolet*.

She went to the people and cried, "Medeo is the *fifolet*! He is slowly killin' us just as he killed those who followed him and never came back. Can't you see that Fifolet will not stop until he gets us all? We have to fight him!"

But the people had no will of their own. They hung their heads in silence; they were afraid. Zula was afraid, too. She feared Fifolet would lead her own children away, never to return. Zula waited and watched until one dark night she saw Medeo enter the corn shed. Softly, softly, she crept up to the shack. Through a crack in the wall she watched as the wizard cast his spell and shed his skin and hid it in a dark corner. Then, before her very eyes, he changed himself into a burning ball of blue and white flames and floated out of the shed.

When Fifolet was long gone, Zula ran back to her *cabane*. She sat on her *galerie*, thinking hard. "How do I fight fire?" she wondered. "How do I fight a *fifolet* fire?"

Suddenly Zula leaped to her feet and ran into her cabin. She filled her deep apron pockets full of the things she would need to fight and, with the help of *le Bon Dieu,* destroy the *fifolet.*

Quietly, Zula slipped into the shed and found the wizard's skin. She shook it out until it hung from her hands like a pair of longjohns flapping from a clothesline. The skin was dry and cool to the touch, like the skin of a lizard. She dipped a hand in her apron pocket and began to scoop something out. Zula quickly filled the wizard's skin to the neck with salt and garlic and a *grand beaucoup,* a big ol' bunch o' *très chaud,* hot, hot, hot cayenne pepper!

Just then she heard a crackling, burning sound at the door. *Vite-vite,* she hid herself in the shadows. The shed was lit up by the eerie, bobbing light of the *fifolet.* Its voice mumbled strange words that Zula had never heard before.

In an instant Medeo was back in his human skin. But all of a sudden that wizard began to itch and twitch, itch and twitch, until he was jumpin' and jitterbuggin' all over the place. He howls out, "Ohhh yeyiiee! Ohhh yeyiiee! I'm burning!" The wizard sees Zula. "You did this!" he screams. "I'm gonna getchoo!"

Medeo's beard was burning with blue-white flames and his eyes glowed like red-hot coals. Thick smoke poured from his nose and ears, and sparks flew from his fingers. Medeo leaped to grab Zula, but as he jumped into the air, he exploded like a firecracker into a roaring fire. "Ohhhh yeyiiee!" In a flash, he burned up to a crisp and all that was left of that mean ol' wizard was a little pile of smoking ash.

The people of the village were free of the *fifolet's* curse. Once again they laughed and danced and sang. To this day they've never been bothered again by any old *fifolet,* 'cause now they know how to fight *fifolet* fire with a *beaucoup* of hot-hot-hot cayenne pepper!

The Half-Man

This story takes me back to my own childhood. Once, when my girlfriend and I were playing out in the swamp woods, we heard an eerie sound coming from the deep, dark thicket. With eyes big as supper plates, we looked at each other and screamed, "Half-Man!" Who would've thought two skinny, knock-kneed, nine-year-old tomboys could run so fast? I'm sure we set a speed record gettin' out of that swamp.

There was once a boy who was just about the stubbornest, most hardheaded thing that ever lived. He didn't pay attention to nothin' anybody told him, no way, no how. He loved to stir up trouble—as long as he didn't get caught. He was the sort of boy who liked to act like he was bigger and braver than everybody else. One night he decided to show the other boys that he was more grown-up than them. "I'm gonna sneak out to the swamp tonight and smoke," he says. "Now who's gonna come with me?" None of the boys wanted to go. "Ah, ya'll are just chicken. I *dare* ya'll. Meet me in the swamp at midnight, or I'll tell everybody ya'll are just a bunch of cowards!"

But the boys wouldn't take the dare. They weren't about to go into that swamp and smoke. Ol' Half-Man might be around!

"Half-Man?" laughs the boy. "Why, ya'll are just big ol' babies! There's no such thing as Half-Man. That's just a story. I'm gonna prove it. I'm gonna spend the whole night out there. Ya'll just watch and see if I come back before mornin'!"

Well, the boy went out into the swamp. There was a full moon and he could see fine and, more important, the boys could see him. He walked deeper and deeper into the swamp woods. At last he stopped and built himself a little fire. He pulled out his tobacco and started smoking. But he wasn't used to the stuff, and he started coughin' and gaggin' like an ol' dog. His face turned green and his stomach was churning like a washing machine. He got dizzy and sick and plopped down on the ground moaning.

Just then, he noticed a thick cloud of smoke rolling out of the swamp woods. "Ah, it's just fog," he thinks. "Wouldn't be no smoke out here like that." He's groaning and moaning and waiting for everything to quit spinning when he hears a strange noise coming from the swamp woods. It was low and rolling, sounded like, "Booogedy-booogedy-boooggedy."

Now most folks would've been makin' tracks by that time, but this boy had moss for brains. He sat there stubborn as a mule. "Those boys are just tryin' to scare me," he thinks. "But I'm not scared of nothin'!"

More smoke is drifting out of the swamp woods now, so thick the boy can barely see. "Funny," he thinks, "this isn't fog—it's smoke. Somethin' must be burnin' some-where and the wind is blowin' this smoke around."

Suddenly, he hears that odd sound again, louder than before: "Booogedy-booogedy-booogedy!"

That boy just keeps sitting there dumb as a duck. Anybody else would've had the sense to get out of there. He's just sitting there, thinking how he's gonna show the other boys up, when all of a sudden a deep rumbling voice right behind him says, "Boooogedy-booogedy-booogedy-booogedy!"

That boy jumps around, and to his horror he sees it's a monster, a monster of a man. It's Half-Man! He rolls up to that boy like a wheel, holding his foot in his one hand, coiled up in a circle. He's blowing thick, smelly smoke rings and hollerin', "Booogedy-booogedy-booogedy!"

He gets up to that boy and unrolls himself, standing up on one leg and glaring out of one red, watery eye. Half-Man was a terrible sight. His half-head was covered with grey, wrinkled skin. His one big eye was bloodshot and squinty. His half-nose was blowing smelly smoke rings, and his half-mouth was full of yellow, stained fangs. Half-Man smelled like a hundred mad skunks!

Ooowhee! That boy was frozen in his tracks. Half-Man reaches out his knotty hand, points a bony finger, and says, "Booogedy-booogedy-booogedy! Give me some smoke or I'll gitchooo!"

That boy was so scared he couldn't move. Half-Man was blowing more smelly smoke rings in the boy's face. He says again, "Booogedy-booogedy-booogedy! Give me some smoke or I'll gitchooo!"

Well, that boy found his feet about then, and took off running like greased lightnin'. But ol' Half-Man just grabs up his foot with that one hand, turns himself into a wheel, and starts rollin' after him, hollerin', "Boogedy-boogedy-boogedy! Give me some smoke or I'll gitchooo!"

Half-Man is getting closer and closer. The boy can feel the monster's hot breath on his back. All of a sudden, he comes up to a bayou. That boy jumps in the water and swims across like he had an outboard motor on his back. Ol' Half-Man couldn't get across so easy. He got bogged down in the mud and just stuck there, spinning like a wheel.

The boy came running out of that swamp faster than a rabbit with his tail on fire, howling like a beat dog, "He got me! He got me! Half-Man got me!" All the boys fell out laughing to see that big ol' bully carrying on so. They never let him boss them around again.

After meeting up with Half-Man, that boy quit all his braggin'. He didn't want to look for trouble anymore; he'd had enough to last him for a good long time. And when he grew into a man and became a *papa,* he'd tell his own son, "Always look out for ol' Half-Man, cause you never know, when you least expect it, he might just sneak up behind ya and—'boogedy-booogedy-booogedy!' Gitchooo!"

The Ghost of Jean Lafitte

Down below New Orleans, the land melts into the salt marshlands of Barataria. It was there among the **chênières**—*the high mounds of shells covered with live oak trees—that Jean Lafitte, the pirate, plied his trade. He made the greatest part of his fortune from the sale of seized human cargoes of African slaves. Legend has it that Lafitte buried his riches and never returned to claim his ill-gotten gain. Countless treasure seekers have dug up Louisiana from New Orleans to the Sabine River, looking for the pirate's long lost riches. When I was a child, kids loved to tell this story, making it as gruesome as possible. This old tale is the only clue to the treasure's location. But treasure hunters beware—the fortune of Jean Lafitte is forever cursed!*

A young, war-weary Confederate soldier was making his long way back home, following the snaking path of a bayou, when a terrible storm fell upon him. The wind wailed as thunder boomed and rain fell like needles. The soldier saw that he had better find shelter, so he left the bayou and began to wander through a thicket. He soon became lost in the blinding rain.

The soldier came to an abandoned house in the middle of nowhere. The door stood open. He called out but nobody answered, and since it was nearly dark he went inside to escape the howling wind. He struck a match and found dry firewood left behind by some other lost soul. The young man quickly made a fire and settled down for the night. He was dead tired from his journey, and he soon fell into a heavy sleep.

Sometime in the deep of the night he waked with the strange feeling that he was not alone in the house. And there by the light of the dying fire, he saw the ghostly figure of a man standing in tall, muddy boots. His arms were folded across his chest and a pirate's cutlass hung at his side.

The man pointed at him and says, "Come with me."

"Who—who are you?" whispers the soldier.

"I am Jean Lafitte," he wails. *"Viens avec moi!* Come with me, save my soul, help me!"

The man disappeared into thin air without another word. The soldier's heart was pounding hard, but he told himself it was only a dream. He stoked the fire and lay back down. The apparition had unsettled him, and now he jumped at every creak and groan of the old house, until at last his tired body gave in to sleep.

The fire had died down when the soldier again waked with a start. A strange, icy draft of wind whistled through the room and the ghostly pirate appeared once more before him.

"Help me, free my soul," the pirate's spirit pleads.

The young man could barely speak for fear. "Wh—what do you wa—want from m—me?" he asks.

"I am condemned," wails the ghost, "a slave to my treasure—bought with human tears and broken hearts. Now I must pay the price of my fortune. My soul is bound to my blood money. Take my treasure and set me freeeee!"

The young man could feel himself being lifted against his will and forced to follow the ghost of Jean Lafitte. The spirit brought him to a secret room. There, with a wave of the pirate's hand, the boards in the floor disappeared to reveal a huge chest, spilling over with treasure. The room was lit up by the shining glow of silver, jewels, and golden coins.

Jean Lafitte stretches out his hands, crying, "Take it! Take my treasure. Help me save my soul!"

The spirit's hands were gory, and bloody tears dripped from his burning eyes. He reached out, closer, closer, until the young man felt the bloodstained fingers grasp his arm like an icy claw—it was the touch of death itself. The soldier's terror rose beyond the power of the spirit's spell and he broke away, running like a madman into the stormy night. The wind tore at him and booming thunder shook the ground. He crashed through the thorny thicket in the blinding rain. Behind him he could hear the ghost crying in the wind, "Take my treasure. Ohhhhh, help meee!"

The young man lived to tell the story, and he warned all who would seek the treasure to beware. The pirate's bloody curse, he would say, follows whoever takes the treasure. To this day, when a storm booms down the bayou, many believe that the wailing wind carries the pitiful cries of the ghost of Jean Lafitte. For his spirit is condemned to wander forever through the dark night, begging, pleading for somebody to take his cursed treasure and free his tortured soul at last.

Knock, Knock, Who's There?

This is a blending of two family stories passed down through my family and told for true. It's a good example of how stories evolve from real events, and survive time and distance to become folktales. The story is based on fact. Buried coffins did indeed float up during flooding—hence the practice of burying the dead above the ground in vaults and "ovens" (wall vaults). According to family legend, one of my ancestors was too cheap to properly bury his wife and, when the land flooded, she floated up and knocked against the house, so terrifying her miserly old husband that he went mad by morning. The rest of the story as I have presented it is based on the further legend of my poor Tante Claire. As the story goes, when she was sixteen, she knocked on her father's door one night, complaining of being sick, but he thought she was just putting on and refused to get her any medical help. By the time he realized just how sick his daughter really was, it was too late. She died on the kitchen table while the unprepared country doctor tried to perform an emergency appendectomy with a butcher knife.

Around La Ville, New Orleans, the land is so low and wet that the dead have to be buried above ground in a vault. Folks don't bury their dead in a grave in the ground. If the river were to overflow the *levée,* or a hurricane to flood the land, your loved one might just float back up from the grave and pay you a return visit!

Down the river a little ways from La Ville, there once lived an old man with his only child, a *jolie fille* called Thérèse. Her *maman* had died and Thérèse was left in the care of her *papa,* a greedy, miserly man who worked his girl like a mule and dressed her in rags. Though she was of a marrying age, he would not allow any young man to court her. She saw no one except her mean ol' *papa.*

All he ever cared for were the gold coins that he kept hidden under a loose board in the floor beneath his bed. Every night he'd lock the door, and by the light of a flickering candle, he'd count his golden coins. He loved the way they clinked and glowed and weighed so heavy in his hands. But poor Thérèse, she was so lonesome. Every night she'd come knocking on his door, knock, knock. Her *papa* would yell out, "Who's there?"

"Papa, *c'est moi,"* she'd say. "It's me, Thérèse. Papa, let me in, talk with me. I am so lonely!"

But her *papa* would only holler back at her, "Girl, get on outta here and get back to work. You only wanta get your hands on my gold, and thatta be over my dead body!"

And so it went until one night, knock, knock. "Who's there?" "Papa, it's me, Thérèse. Me, I'm sick-sick," she moans. "Papa, let me in!"

But he just yells back, "You lazy good-for-nothin'! Get outta here. You're not sick. You just wanta get your hands on my money, and thatta be over my dead body!"

Again and again Thérèse returned to her father's door, knock, knock.

"Who's there?"

"Papa, *c'est moi*. Papa, let me in. I'm bad sick. I need the healer. Please, Papa, send for the *traiteur!*"

Knock, knock.

"Who's there?"

"Papa, please help me. The pain is worse. Oh, Papa, open the door!"

But her *papa's* heart was as cold as his golden coins. At last the girl's cries faded to silence, and she knocked no more. The old man was full of curiosity, and so he opened the door. There, lying lifeless on the porch floor, was *jolie* Thérèse.

The old man was too stingy to buy a vault for his daughter. Instead, he laid Thérèse in a crude wooden coffin and buried her in a shallow, swampy grave down by the cypress tree. The neighbors all shook their heads. They warned there would be trouble. How could poor Thérèse rest in peace in such a grave?

Three weeks went by and a storm began to coil up out over the gulf. The winds churned and rain fell like needles as the hurricane passed over the land. Night found the old man sitting in his room counting his gold coins by flickering candlelight.

Outside, the wind howled and blew sheets of rain against the house. The old man did not know that the river had already spilled over the *levée* and sent its dark water across the land. He sat in his rocking chair, his lap full of gold, rocking and counting, *"Un, deux, trois ..."*

Something thumped against his porch with a hollow wooden clatter. Knock, knock, knock sounded at his door.

"Who's there?" he hollers.

Only a great sigh like the wind answered. "Just a loose shutter bangin'," he thinks, and went on counting his shining gold. *"Un, deux, trois ..."*

Knock, knock, knock pounded at his door, stronger this time.

"Who's there?"

Only a whining wind answered him. "Just that good-for-nothin' hound dog tryin' to get in," he thinks. Again he returned to his golden coins. *"Un, deux, trois ..."*

Knock, knock, knock! Three great booming knocks hammered at his door.

"Who's there?"

Only a low, sad moaning. A cold shiver ran down the old man's back. "Storm's gotcha all jumpy," he says to himself. "It's just the wind blowin' that ol' live oak tree, scrapin' its branches against the house."

But the moaning rose and rose above the wailing wind until it became a horrifying scream.

"Papa, *c'est moi,* Thérèse! Let me in! It's me, Thérèse!" Knock, knock, knock! "Papa, let me in!" Knock, knock, knock! "Papa, let me innnnnn!"

As the eye of the storm passed over the house, a bloodcurdling shriek pierced the deadly calm.

Three days passed and the waters receded. Neighbors came by to look in on the old man. They rode onto his land, and as they passed by the cypress tree they saw that the flood had washed all the dirt away from Thérèse's grave and it was empty.

They knocked at the back door but no voice answered. Fearing some harm had befallen the old man, they went inside. They found him sitting like stone in his rocking chair, cold as marble, his hair gone snow white. A silent scream was frozen on his face, and his eyes bulged in glassy terror.

Across the room, the door hung limp from one hinge, as though some monstrous fist had pounded it down. Before it lay a battered, splintered coffin and, inside, the gruesome corpse of Thérèse. Her withered hands clutched her *papa's* golden coins, and a ghastly smile lay fixed upon her decaying lips.

With the money, the neighbors bought Thérèse a whitewashed vault and gave her a proper aboveground burial. There was not enough money to buy the old man a vault, so they buried him in a pine coffin down by the cypress tree. Since that time, whenever the river threatens to flood the land, the old man's troubled spirit rises to warn all that danger is at hand. Folks know he's payed them a visit when they hear someone knock, knock, knocking at their door but nobody is ever there!

The Singing Bones

My grandmother was what some people might call super-stitious. I like to think she was just cautious. I heard this tale from her and have encountered versions of it in nursing homes and schoolyards. Recently a friend of mine had an experience which gave me a new slant on this story. He was visiting a cemetery late in the evening when he heard music coming from one of the vaults. He says he lit a rag gettin' outta there! The next morning he was full of curiosity, so he went back. Among the vaults he found the source of the music—an electronic greeting card which, when opened, played "You Are My Sunshine." The wind must have blown it open—right?

There was once a widower who had twenty-five children. For true, he had so many children that he lost count of them. Their poor *maman* had died and the family couldn't get along without her. Papa couldn't work and care for the children too, so he looked for a new wife. But the only woman who would have him was an ugly ol' thing with a sharp tongue and a heart cold as stone. He married her anyway. After all, a poor man with so many children can't be too choosey. The children soon found their *belle-mère* to be cruel. Little by little she took the money her husband gave her for food and secretly buried it under a big rock. The children began to complain of hunger, for she only gave them a little rice each day. Belle-Mère whipped the children hard for their complaints, and they soon learned to suffer in silence. Papa came home after the children were asleep. He ate his good supper never knowing that his children went hungry. It wasn't long before Belle-Mère begrudged the children even the little food she had been giving them. She began to think of some way that she could take even more money for herself.

"My husband is so blind," she thinks, "he doesn't even know how many children he has! There must surely be a way I can keep him fed and hide away more money for myself. When I have a nice nest egg laid by, I'll leave him and his whinin' brats. Then it'll be too late for him to do anything to stop me."

Now, one day Papa came home as usual, hungry and too tired to take much notice of his wife or ask after his children. Belle-Mère served him his supper of rice, beans, and meat with no bones. It seemed to him the meat had an unusual taste.

"How is it that this meat has no bones?" he asks.

"Bones are heavy; meat is cheaper without bones," says Belle-Mère.

Papa ate quietly for a while. "Why is it you don't eat?" he asks his wife.

"I have no teeth. How can you expect me to eat meat without teeth?"

"That is true," he says. Papa didn't say anything else for fear of making his wife mad, for she was as hot-tempered as she was ugly.

Papa seldom saw all twenty-five of his children at one time. A few would always be running here or there, so he didn't notice if a few were gone. In truth, he took little notice of his extra-large family.

One Sunday morning the house seemed quieter than usual. Thinking the children must be up to no good, he called them to him. But there were only four pairs of twins, two sets of triplets, and one toddler.

"Where are the others?" he asks Belle-Mère.

"What others?" she asks.

"It seems to me I have many more children than these," he says with a frown.

"You do not even know how many children you have, and you ask me where they are? If you care so much, they've gone to see their *grandmaman,*" she says, "to help the poor ol' thing with her chores. They'll be back in a few weeks."

This didn't seem strange to Papa as the children often visited their *grandmaman.* He said no more about it, not caring to throw his wife into a rage.

Things went on as before. Papa left early and returned late, too tired to ask about his children. Belle-Mère served him his supper of rice, beans, and meat without bones. One night he again grew curious about the flavor of the meat.

"Wife," he asks, "what kind of meat is this? I never tasted meat like this before."

Belle-Mère flew into a rage. "First you complain there aren't any bones, when I am only tryin' to save money.

Now you're complainin' about my cookin'. Well, if you don't like it, then you can just buy the meat and cook it yourself!"

Papa was too tired to argue with Belle-Mère and her sharp tongue, so he just let the matter drop. Anyway, the meat wasn't bad-tasting, just unusual.

He ate his supper, thinking, "She's right, the house and the children are her business. Why should I be concerned with woman's work?"

The days passed, and each night Papa ate his supper of rice, beans, and meat with no bones. He didn't ask any more questions about the meat or his children. But one Sunday morning he got to thinking that the house was deathly quiet.

"Now what are those children up to? It's way too quiet. Come children, come to your *papa!*" he calls.

One by one the children began to appear, as though they had been hiding in the cracks. Papa soon saw something was wrong, though. There were only one set of twins and the youngest child.

"Where are your brothers and sisters?" he asks.

The children looked at their stepmother with frightened eyes and said nothing.

"Old man," snaps Belle-Mère, "are you complaining again? The children are visiting their *grandmaman,* of course. They will be back in a few weeks. Now hush and stop botherin' us with questions!"

After supper, Papa sat out on a big rock under a great live oak tree, enjoying his evening rest. He watched his three children playing quietly under the tree. They seemed so sad and so thin! He began to think of his other children and how he missed their games and laughter. He was on the point of going to get them from their *grandmaman* when suddenly he heard his missing children singing sweetly. Their voices seemed to come from far away.

"The children are on their way back home," he thinks happily.

The singing grew louder until he could make out the words of their song:

> *Our stepmother killed us,*
> *Our **papa** ate us,*
> *We are not in a coffin,*
> *We are not in the cemetery,*
> *Holy, holy, holy.*

Papa thought his ears were failing him. "What kind of song is this?" he thinks. He calls the children, "Come to Papa, my little ones. Tell me why you sing such a strange song!"

The sweet voices started singing again, closer and louder than before:

> *Our stepmother killed us,*
> *Our **papa** ate us,*
> *We are not in a coffin,*
> *We are not in the cemetery,*
> *Holy, holy, holy.*

The singing seemed to surround Papa, to flow from the very stone he sat upon. He got down on his knees and put his ear to the rock. Once again he heard his children singing, sweet as angels:

Our stepmother killed us,
*Our **papa** ate us,*
We are not in a coffin,
We are not in the cemetery,
Holy, holy, holy.

With trembling hands, Papa rolled the stone away. To his horror, there lay a great mound of small human bones, half-buried in the earth. The bones began to sing:

Our stepmother killed us,
*Our **papa** ate us,*
We are not in a coffin,
We are not in the cemetery,
Holy, holy, holy.

Bitter tears fell from Papa's eyes and his heart broke as he realized the truth: his cruel wife had killed the children and cooked them, and he had eaten them, his own flesh and blood! He fell on his knees, crying, "Ah, my children, forgive me! Why didn't I ask about you? Why didn't I watch out for you like a good father? I shoulda seen what was happenin'."

Papa leaped to his feet with murder in his heart. "Belle-Mère," he screams, "you're gonna pay for my children's lives!"

He ran up to the house, but he was too late. When Belle-Mère heard the singing and knew that she had been discovered, she slipped out by the back door and ran down to the rock where her money was buried. She meant to dig it up and escape. She clawed through the dirt around the the children's bones, frantic for her money.

Suddenly, the bones began to sing, louder and louder like the wailing wind of a storm, until the ground rumbled and split. The sky opened up and heaven's fury broke loose upon her. A mighty lightning bolt struck Belle-Mère right between her eyes with a boomin' crack! The wicked woman exploded into a heap of dust.

Gradually the storm beat itself out and a warm rain began to fall, like teardrops from heaven, washing away the dust until the children's bones were white as snow and no trace remained of the evil *belle-mère*.

Papa put his children's bones in a coffin and buried it in the cemetery beside the grave of their true mother. For the rest of his life he never again touched meat, haunted by the meat that had no bones. He lived in great sorrow for his murdered children, and his heart was heavy with his own guilt. He wished to be released from his burden, and he prayed for death, but heaven punished him instead with a very long life.

The Ring and the Rib

When I was a little girl, I would often accompany Miss Irene down to the shotgun-style Catholic church that served our little country community. On Saturdays we'd clean the church and get it ready for mass. I loved the statues of the saints and the smell of the wax, but the place made me a little uneasy, too. One day I got scared while Miss Irene was in the back room. I thought there was a ghost in the church. Instead of telling me there were no such things as ghosts, Miss Irene told me this story. It is my favorite ghost story to this day, and the memory of Miss Irene telling it to me can warm up the darkest, gloomiest place.

It was a stormy, gray Saturday morning when Irene, the widow woman, went to clean the church. Irene was a poor woman and couldn't afford to put but a few *sous* into the collection basket on Sundays. Still, she did what she could. She cleaned and polished the church floors until the old wood glowed. She brought deep red roses and creamy gardenias from her own bushes for the altar, and their sweet scent mixed with the warm smell of wax and candles. Her work turned the plain little church into a place of beauty and hope.

The building was made of whitewashed boards and built shotgun-style. No fancy stained glass here, only square panes of blue-colored glass in the windows. The sanctuary was as simple and unadorned as the poor people of the village themselves: old handmade pews worn smooth with age; an embroidered altar cloth; and the statues of the saints, once brightly painted, now fading with age.

On that morning, Irene lit the candles and a lamp, for the storm made the little church darker than usual. As she worked in the stillness of the room, a clap of thunder in the distance caused the boardframe church to tremble, and a shiver ran down her back. She had the uneasy feeling that she was not alone, that something or someone was hiding in the shadows. She listened but heard nothing.

"Just the storm comin' up," she thinks. "This ol' church is always full of squeaks and creaks when there's a strong wind blowin'."

She worked on but could not get over the feeling that somebody was looking over her shoulder. Yet as often as she glanced about, she saw nothing. Then all of a sudden, a cold breeze touched her neck like the grip of an icy hand. She spun around to see a figure step out of the shadows!

It was a tall, bony man with a pale face and eyes that seemed to burn right through her. He wore high boots caked with mud, and his clothing was torn and dirty. In his side, from a bloody, gaping wound, a single bony rib glinted in the candlelight.

"Mon Dieu!" she whispers, clutching her rosary beads. "Help me, help me!" Her heart throbbed in her throat as the ghostly man slowly approached. He stretches out his bony pale hands and moans, *"Sauvez mon âme.* Help me! My soul can not rest. Please help me!" Tears flowed from his burning eyes and fell on the polished wood floor.

Irene was frozen with fear, but at last she found her voice and whispers, "What do you want from me?"

"I have been murdered! I cannot rest in peace until justice is done. Find my murderer. Bury me."

"Spirit, who killed you?" the woman asks.

"It was Villien," the spirit moans. "Villien murdered me. Find him! Lay my bones to rest. I am so weary, so tired. Help me!"

"Villien," she whispers, "he's the richest man in the parish. He owns everything. Nobody will believe a ghost told me this. They'll say I'm crazy. Villien will run me out of the parish! I've got children. We'll have no place to go. We'll starve. No, spirit, I can't help you, I'm afraid."

But the ghost says, "Don't be afraid. I will help you. Hold out your hand."

Irene obeyed, and the spirit dropped something shiny in her palm: a golden ring. He held out his own pale hand and whispers, "Give me your gold wedding ring."

The woman took the ring from her trembling hand and offered it. The ghost moans, "You must help me. Find Villien. Bury me!"

"Spirit, where are your bones hidden?" she asks.

"I will reveal the place when the time is right. Go now!" And with that, the ghost disappeared.

Irene waited in the dark church for a long time while the thunder continued to pound and blue lightning flashed through the windows. Was she dreaming? But the golden ring glowed in her hand, and on the floor the spirit's teardrops sparkled like dewdrops in the candlelight. Finally the storm rumbled away and a gentle rain began to fall. Irene hurried to the village. She stopped before the office of *le grand shérif.* Her heart still beat hard, but the golden ring clenched in her fist gave her confidence as she stepped inside to tell her strange story.

"Shérif," she says, "a man has been murdered. You gotta come right away!"

"What's this? A man murdered?" he asks, jumping up from his chair. "What man? Where is the body?"

"I don't know what man," Irene says, shaking her head, "and I don't know where the body is hidden."

The sheriff looks at Irene in amazement. "What do you mean, you don't know the murdered man and you don't know where the body is? How do you know there's been a murder?"

Irene looked him straight in the eyes and says, "I know a man was murdered because his ghost appeared before me in the church and told me so. The ghost said that Villien was the murderer."

"What? Woman have you gone moon-mad? Villien? You must think I'm crazy, too!" the sheriff hollers. "You think I'm gonna arrest Villien, the richest man in the parish, with no proof, no evidence, no body?"

"The spirit gave me something to show you."

Irene held out the golden ring. The sheriff took the ring, turning it 'round and 'round. Three initials had been carved inside the ring, the initials of a man who had disappeared five years ago.

"You say you found this ring at the church?" he asks.

"No," says Irene, "I said the ghost of a murdered man gave it to me, and he took my wedding ring. He begged for help. Said, 'Find my body. Bury me.' Said Villien killed him."

"Something strange is goin' on for true out at that church," the sheriff says, "and I mean to get to the bottom of it!"

The *grand shérif* rounded up a group of men. They gathered up shovels and buckets and headed for the church. By the time they reached the little shotgun building, the rain had let up. The men began to dig all around the church, but their shovels didn't turn up a thing.

Back in the village, the story spread like wildfire until it reached the ears of Villien himself. His blood boiling, he saddled his horse and rode like the wind to the church.

Villien pulled his horse to a stop and glared at Irene. "You accuse me of murder? Where is the body? You have no proof!" he hisses. "Woman, you be outta my parish by sundown, you and your brats. I don't care where you go. You can starve for all I care! Nobody accuses Villien of murder and stays in my parish. Nobody will help you. They'll do as I say. They all work for me. I own them and their pitiful little village."

The men all stopped digging, for they were afraid of Villien.

"There's nothing buried out here," they cried. "This woman is mad. Nobody's been murdered." And they commenced to load up their tools.

Just then a voice whispered in Irene's ear, "Look under the church. Dig under the church."

"Dig under the church!" she calls out. "Quick! Look under the church. The spirit told me."

The men looked at each other and grumbled, but the sheriff ordered them to start digging under the church as the woman said.

Villien starts screaming, "Stop that diggin'! Sheriff, if you wanta keep that badge, tell your men to stop."

But the sheriff only hollered out, "Keep diggin!"

The little church was built up on rock pilings. Underneath, the air was musty and the ground was muddy. The men dug as best they could in the tight space. Suddenly, one of them gave out a shout that his shovel had struck something hard under the altar. Lifting his shovel into the light, he found a skull staring back at him.

Everyone was shouting with excitement and disbelief as they pulled out the remainder of the skeleton from its shallow grave. But a sudden quiet fell over them.

"There!" someone said, pointing.

"What is it?"

Something was shining through the dirt that clung to the skeleton. The sheriff carefully brushed the earth away. There, just as Irene had said, was her golden wedding ring, twisted tightly onto one bony rib.

The sheriff ordered the arrest of Villien. Terrified by the dead man's ghost, Villien confessed in full and found his justice at the end of a rope.

The villagers buried the skeleton in the cemetery, but it is said that the ghost continues to haunt the church. On Saturday mornings, women still come to wax and polish and set out roses and gardenias to glorify the altar. Now and then a cold shiver is felt, and they peer into the shadows and retell the story of the rib and the ring. Are they afraid? *Mais non.* It is a good spirit that watches over the poor little church, protecting all who come in need or trouble. Those who enter in peace have nothing to fear.

Glossary

Words

- **âme** soul; spirit

- **ami** friend

- **banane** banana

- **beaucoup** a lot

- **bébé** baby

- **belle** beautiful

- **belle-mère** stepmother

- **beau-père** stepfather

- **bon (m.); bonne (f.)** good

- **bonheur** good fortune

- **boscoyo** cypress knees; protruding roots of a cypress tree

- **cabane** cabin, shack

- **café au lait** coffee with an equal part of milk

- **carencro** buzzard

- *chaud* hot

- *chênière* oak grove

- *cher (m.); chère (f.)* dear

- *chien* dog

- *cocodrie* alligator

- *couche-couche* steamed, moist cornmeal eaten as a cereal

- *de pomme* apple; some apple

- *deux* two

- *diable* devil

- *Dieu* God

- *fais-dodo* all-night dance

- *femme* woman; wife

- *fève* bean, pea

- *fille* girl

- *gaime* rooster

- *galerie* front porch

- *goujon* mud catfish; yellow catfish

- *graisse* grease

- *grand (m.); grande (f.)* great or big

- *grandmaman* grandmother

- *gris-gris* charm; spell

- *gumbo ya-ya* everybody talks at once

- *joie de vivre* joy of living

- *jolie* pretty

- *la Louisianne* Louisiana

- *lapin* rabbit

- *La Ville* New Orleans

- *les petits* the little ones; small children

- *levée* river or bayou bank; built-up bank; rising

- *loup-garou* werewolf

- *Madame* Mrs.; Ma'am

- *maison* house

- *malin* tricky

- *maman* mama

- *Mamselle* Miss

- *mangeur de poulet* chicken hawk

- *Mardi Gras* carnival held just before Lent celebrated with masks, parades, music, food, and dance

- *mon (m.); ma (f.)* my

- *mort* death

- *mouche à feu* firefly

- *mousse* moss

- ***M'su; Monsieur*** Mr.

- ***non*** no

- ***orimomo*** a little chant, like "lah-dee-dah"

- ***ours*** bear

- ***pacane*** pecan

- ***padnat*** buddy; friend

- ***papa*** papa; daddy

- ***parrain*** godfather

- ***pauvre*** poor

- ***pichou*** bobcat

- ***pourquoi*** why

- ***p'tite*** little; little one

- ***raconteur*** storyteller

- ***shérif*** sheriff

- ***sirop*** syrup

- ***sou*** cent

- ***tasso*** dried strips of meat; jerky

- ***taureau*** bull

- ***traiteur*** healer

- ***très*** very

- ***trois*** three

- ***un (m.); une (f.)*** one, a, an

- ***vite*** quick; fast

Phrases

- ***bonne chance*** good luck

- ***ça va?*** how's it going?

- ***ça va mal*** it's going bad; not good

- ***c'est bon*** that's good; this is good

- ***c'est moi*** it's me

- ***c'est tout*** that's it; that's all

- ***c'est vrai*** that's true

- ***comment ça va?*** how's it going?

- ***mais jamais*** but never

- ***mais non*** but no; of course not

- ***mais oui*** but of course; yes

- ***merci beaucoup*** thank you very much

- ***mon Dieu*** my God

- ***pas du tout*** not at all

- ***viens avec moi*** come with me